TILLY SAT BOLT UPRIGHT IN BED
AND GAVE HIM A VIOLENT PUSH.

"Don't touch me!" she gasped. "You don't l-love m-me at all. You're only obeying your father's will. This is nothing more than another business contract. Oh, God, I'm so ashamed."

"Don't be a ninny," said the marquess, trying to take her in his arms. "You love me, don't you?"

With that last sentence the marquess proved he was not the expert lover, the Don Juan he had fondly believed himself to be. Had he said "I love you," Tilly might have forgiven him. But as it was, she crouched up against the bedhead and glared at him with the savagery of a wildcat.

"Get out!" she yelled. "OUT! OUT! OUT!"

Also by Marion Chesney writing as Jennie Tremaine:

DAISY

LUCY

POLLY

MOLLY

GINNY

TILLY

Jennie Tremaine

Marion Chesney writing as
Jennie Tremaine

A DELL BOOK

Published by
Dell Publishing Co., Inc.
1 Dag Hammarskjold Plaza
New York, New York 10017

Extract from MANNERS FOR WOMEN by Mrs. Humphreys
published by Webb & Bower (Publishers) Ltd., Exeter, England,
1979.

Dell ® TM 681510, Dell Publishing Co., Inc.

ISBN: 0-440-18637-4

Printed in the United States of America

One Previous Edition

December 1987

10 9 8 7 6 5 4 3 2 1

WFH

For Sally and Michael Murphy
and their sons, Conal and Gavin,
with love

TILLY

CHAPTER ONE

The Honorable Miss Matilda Burningham paced the smooth lawns of her family estate on all the perfect glory of an early spring morning and bitterly envied the peace of nature. Blossoms frothed in a sea of pink-and-white waves in the orchard, daffodils blazed gold under the old trees on the lawns, and the sweet, heady exotic smell of hyacinth floated on the slight breeze. A blackbird at her feet cocked its glossy head, looking for worms. All was as it had been—on the outside at least.

King Edward, accompanied by his stupendous retinue, had departed, leaving Jeebles, the rambling ancestral home of the Burninghams, to relapse into its usual rural torpor. But inside, Matilda—Tilly to her few friends—were stirring faint, uncomfortable pricklings of unease. She was *glad* to get back into her customary dress of old riding breeches and jersey, she told herself. The royal visit had forced her into fashionable clothes for the first and, she hoped, the last time in her life.

Tilly was only just seventeen years old and still carried around a layer of puppy fat that was slow to melt because of Tilly's fondness for nursery teas. But she had done her best to please her father, Lord Charles Burningham, who had nearly had an apoplexy over the excitement of the king's visit.

A lady's maid had been hired specially to try to turn Tilly into a swan. Tilly's skin still itched at the memory of the layers of clothes she had had to put on.

To begin with there was a garment known as a "combination," a kind of vest and pants in one piece, made of fine wool with legs reaching to the knee. Over this had gone a corset made of pink coutil with busks fastening down the front and tight lacing at the back to produce a fashionable swanlike figure. To accentuate the bust and hips, silk pads were attached under the arms and at the hips. Then came a camisole or petticoat-bodice that buttoned down the front and was trimmed with lace around the neck and had diminutive puffed sleeves. Then came the knickers that had lace frills at the knee and buttoned at the waist. Then the steel-gray silk stockings that were clipped to the corset, and then the vast and rustling petticoat.

A blouse and skirt had been deemed suitable day wear for Tilly and proved to be an added torture. The junction of the skirt and blouse was concealed by a stiffened belt that fastened at the front with a clasp and at the back was pinned to the undergarments so that never an unladylike gap would show. Going to the lavatory had been turned into a full-scale military operation, reflected Tilly with a sigh.

She had been placed next to King Edward at the dining table. She had been told that the king liked to listen rather than talk, and Tilly had tried hard. But she was unused to making social conversation, and a cloud of boredom had soon settled over the royal brow. "Old Tum-Tum," as the gourmand king was called, began to peevishly rattle his cutlery and drum his fingers on the table, a familiar sign that he was displeased with his partner. So poor Tilly had been supplanted by a dazzling charmer who had not even had her first Season, Lady Aileen Dunbar.

Tilly had always been rather scornful of frilly, fussy, and twittery girls like Lady Aileen, but she had to admit that she did envy her during the royal visit. And not only because of the king's flattering attention to Lady Aileen, but because of the interest shown to the silly girl by none other than the Marquess of Heppleford. The marquess was designed like a Greek god with thick fair hair, sleepy blue eyes, and a classic profile. He was just over six feet tall and was accounted to be the finest shot and huntsman in all of England. Tilly, who was a keen huntswoman herself, longed for the handsome marquess's notice. But, no. He only had eyes for Lady Aileen. Rats!

Tilly moodily kicked at a piece of manicured turf and turned her mind away from that particular worry to another. How on earth had her father managed to *pay* for all this magnificence. An extra wing had had to be built to house the royal servants, the library had been wrenched apart and rebuilt as a bowling alley to pander to the current royal fad, and then there was the food—the lobster, the quail—and the rare vintage wines, the champagne!

Since the departure of King Edward, her father had been closeted for long hours with his steward, only emerging from the estates office for meals, and each time he seemed to have grown older and more worried. But to all Tilly's anxious queries he would only conjure up a thin smile and ruffle her carroty curls and say, "Don't worry, my son. We shall come about."

Lord Charles could be forgiven for often forgetting that Tilly was not a boy. She had faithfully dressed and behaved like the son he had always longed for, with the sad result that the marriageable young men of the county referred to her as "a good sport," and her former girl friends, who had lately blossomed into ribbons and bows and whispers and giggles, now shuddered and said Tilly smelled of the stables.

Tilly set off on her rounds of her tenants, trying to banish the feeling that she had woken up on this spring morning to find that she was, well, somehow *odd*. She briefly wondered what her mother, who had died when Tilly was a baby, had been like and then pushed that thought aside as she headed for the South Lodge to inquire after the lodge keeper, Mr. Pomfret's, weak chest.

Mrs. Pomfret looked none too pleased to see Tilly, as she was surrounded by stacks of clothes waiting to be ironed and had three small children clamoring and clutching at her skirts, but nonetheless she dropped Tilly a low curtsy and replied politely that Mr. Pomfret was "coming along remarkable."

"I told him he shouldn't have been out in that damp weather we had," said Tilly. "I shall bring him some of my own medicine from the stillroom."

"Well, I don't know but that what the doctor's given Fred ain't the best thing—"

"Nonsense!" said Tilly brusquely. "I know what's best for him. I'll bring it along tomorrow. Goodness, I'm parched. Any chance of a cup of tea?"

"Of course, miss," cried Mrs. Pomfret. "I'll put the kettle on."

Tilly stretched out a booted foot toward the hearth with a sigh of satisfaction. Mrs. Pomfret made very good tea indeed. It never crossed Tilly's mind that Mrs. Pomfret had more to do with her time than make tea. Tilly had been treated like visiting royalty by the tenants and the servants for as long as she could remember. Like many of her peers, she had fallen into the habit of believing that she alone knew best what to do for them.

She enjoyed living her tenants lives for them and genuinely believed she was bringing a little glamour and excitement into their mundane existences by her frequent visits.

There was the rattle of carriage wheels on

the gravel outside the lodge and Mrs. Pomfret turned around with a cluck of dismay, wiping her hands on her apron. "I'd better go open the gates, seeing as how Fred is poorly," she said.

"I'll go," said Tilly, bounding to her feet and surprising both herself and Mrs. Pomfret. "You attend to the tea."

Thrusting her hands in her breeches pockets, Tilly strolled out to the massive iron gates. Her bright-red hair was shoved up under a boy's riding hat and she screwed up her eyes to see who was in the carriage, a mannerism she had caught from her father, which dully prevented the world from finding out that the Honorable Matilda had an exceedingly fine pair of large blue eyes.

A brougham was drawn up at the gates, pulled by a spanking pair of glossy chestnuts. A liveried coachman in a spun-glass wig stared down at Tilly from his box.

"Open the gates, lad," he called to Tilly. Tilly stood staring with her mouth open. Looking out of the window of the carriage was the exquisite and handsome Marquess of Heppleford.

"Come along," said the coachman. "Damned inbreeding," he added under his

15

breath, making the footman on the back strap snigger and Tilly turn as red as fire.

Tilly swung open the heavy gates and stood aside as the brougham rolled past. The marquess's cold gray eyes stared indifferently at her and then, it seemed, through her.

Tilly swung the gates shut again and made her way slowly back to the lodge. Should she have told that cheeky coachman exactly who she was? But for the first time in her life, Tilly began to feel vaguely uncomfortable about her own appearance and a vision of the sparkling and lovely Lady Aileen flashed before her eyes. The coachman would never have mistaken Lady Aileen for a lodge boy. But then Lady Aileen would never have lowered herself to opening the lodge gates!

Worse was in store for the Honorable Tilly. As she walked around to the back of the lodge and into the kitchen, Mrs. Pomfret's voice from the bedroom above carried down the stairs with fatal clarity. "I dunno that I should have let Miss Tilly open those gates, and that's a fact, Fred. But then there never was any use in telling her anything nohow. She means well, but she do take up a body's time, asking for tea, and me with the ironing to do and the kids to feed. Thinks she's doing us a favor, Fred, and that's a fact. Bessie Jenkins down by the Five Mile says as how even when the king was here, she had Miss Tilly sprawled around her kitchen for a whole afternoon, telling her how to make seedcake—as if Bessie hadn't been making it since the day Miss Tilly was born. And why don't she dress like a lady?" Mrs. Pomfret's voice dropped to a murmur and Tilly stood on the cold flags of the kitchen floor as if turned to stone.

She had felt she had been doing something worthwhile in visiting the tenants, thinking that they looked forward to her calls as much as she did herself. The kettle began to sing on the hob and Tilly gave it an agonized stare, as if it, too, were going to accuse her of time-wasting. She gave a little gulp and turned and ran from the lodge, up the graveled drive, cutting across the lawns to where the mellow pile of Jeebles lay basking in the morning sun.

There had been Burninghams at Jeebles for as long as anyone could remember. Perhaps in the days before the Norman Conquest there had actually been a Saxon called Jeebles to give the house its name, but if there had, there was not even a tombstone to mark his passing. The huge mansion was a conglomeration of different architecture that time and ivy had blended into a harmonious whole.

Tilly scuttled quickly up the back stairs to her bedroom and then marched up to the long looking glass and stared at her reflection. She had a shapely, if immature, plump figure. Tendrils of carroty hair escaped from under her riding helmet and her wide, brilliant blue eyes, for once uncrinkled, stared back at her in dismay. She was blessed with a creamy English complexion, unusual in a redhead, but it was already unbecomingly and unfashionably tanned.

She slowly pulled off her riding helmet and gazed in disgust at the rioting mass of red curls, unfashionably soft and round, not frizzled like those of the ladies in the fashion plates.

"I don't like me," said Tilly miserably. "I look like a freak . . . I pester the tenants . . . I wish I were a man. If I were a man, Heppleford wouldn't look at me. He won't look at me anyway. Oh, I wish . . ." But all these new agonies were so bewildering that Tilly did not know exactly what she wished.

It was not as if Tilly had never contemplated marriage. On her eighteenth birthday, she knew she would be "brought out" and have a Season in London, like other girls of her class. She would endure the hell of corsets and skirts until such time as some jolly good sort would propose, whereupon they would agree to give up all this London nonsense and retire to the country, where they would hunt amicably from morning to night. Tilly had been kissed after the hunt only the previous winter. Tommy Bryce-James, one of the local lads, had drunk too much champagne and had staggered with her behind some trees at the edge of the woods and had planted a wet kiss on her mouth. It had not been a particularly enjoyable experience, but Tilly vaguely gathered it was something that women either got used to or, if they could not, they shut their eyes and thought of the Empire.

The Marquess of Heppleford had seen her attired in a bewildering variety of clothes, since, during a royal visit, it was forbidden for any lady to appear in the same ensemble twice. But he hadn't noticed her. Drat it! Tonight, she would go down to the drawing room exactly as she was. Other fellows considered her a good sort. It was as much as she could hope that the marquess would think the same.

Lord Philip, Marquess of Heppleford, looked rather anxiously at his host from under drooping lids. Lord Charles was not looking very well, although the man was only around fifty. His hair was already gray and the skin of his face was crisscrossed with lines of red, broken veins. His clothes hung loosely on his slight figure and his blue eyes held a lost look like that of a stray dog.

"So I happened to be in the neighborhood," said the marquess, "and thought I would drop in and see how you were getting along after Kingie's visit. My father suffered one of his visits, you know, and the old bank balance was bloody well near zero by the time he left. Just as bad as having Henry the Eighth landing in on one."

Lord Charles leaned forward eagerly. "And how did your father cope? The bank balance, I mean."

"Oh, he had various stocks and things that came up trumps. You in difficulties, Charles?"

"Well, I am rather," said Lord Charles gloomily. "I've already had to sell off the property in Scotland, and then the hunting box in Yorkshire had to go. Trouble is, I invested in all the wrong things and the

20

worse things got, the worse I invested. The king's visit was the last straw."

"You could have refused," said the marquess lazily. "Told old Tum-Tum you'd turned Methodist or Christian Scientist or something. Freddie Barminster was threatened with the royal presence, so he sent a pile of tracts entitled 'The End of the World Is at Hand' and stuff like that to Buck House and informed His Majesty that he, Freddie, had found this splendid new religion and was just waiting for a chance to convert the monarch. Visit was canceled like a shot."

"When the king of England honors me with a personal visit, I would think it unpatriotic and *caddish* to refuse," said Lord Charles stiffly.

"I'm not turning Bolshevist, you know," said the marquess mildly. "But with my father's death, I inherited the title and the responsibilities. I've got a duty to my servants and tenants and I assure you, if His Majesty showed any signs whatsoever of honoring me with his presence, I would plead leprosy or anything else I could think of."

"I envy you," sighed Lord Charles. "But with old buffers like me, the monarch must always come first." He looked up as the door opened. "Come in, my boy," he said warmly.

"Here's Lord Philip kindly dropped in to see us."

Lord Philip turned and tried not to stare. It was the boy from the lodge . . . no, it must be Charles's son . . . no, by God, it was that weird daughter of his. What was her name? . . . Tilly . . . that was it.

He rose to his feet and made Tilly a graceful bow. He took her small hand to kiss it and found to his surprise that his own was being wrung in a knuckle-cracking handshake. A pair of large, beautiful eyes looked up into his own and then Tilly's unfortunate mannerism of crinkling up her eyes took over. The marquess led Tilly over to a sofa and set himself to charm. He prided himself on his social manners and, after all, he was fond of old Charles. He therefore smiled dazzlingly into what he could see of Tilly's eyes and asked her in his light, lazy voice whether she was looking forward to her Season.

"Oh, I shan't be out this year," said Tilly, slumping into the chesterfield as if she wished its down-stuffed depths would hide her. "But I suppose I shall have to go through with all that rot next year."

"Come, now," teased the marquess. "Surely you will enjoy all the balls and parties and all the young men paying court to you."

Tilly gave a loud, embarrassed laugh. "I'd really rather hunt than do anything," she said, and then her face brightened. "I hear you are a capital huntsman. You must tell me some of your experiences."

"Perhaps, later," said the marquess gently. He privately thought women were a nuisance on the hunting field, always getting their long skirts tangled in the branches. Not that this specimen of English womanhood seemed to bother with skirts—and more shame to her! Eccentricity was all very well in the middle-aged. In girls, it was painful. He averted his eyes slightly and wished he had not come. And yet . . . there was a strange, restless magnetism about this impossible girl. It was a pity. . . . But that was as far as his thoughts about Tilly went, for Lord Charles gently claimed his attention.

Tilly made her escape. She had decided to change the slightly bored look on Lord Philip's face. She would put on her best shirtwaister for luncheon—for surely the marquess would stay for lunch.

With the help of one of the housemaids, she managed to get into her corset, her skirt and her blouse with its uncomfortable high-boned collar. With great daring, she heated up the curling tongs and frizzled the front of her hair. Then she was liberally doused in something the housemaid referred to as Oh-Dick-Alone, and smelling exotically of cologne and burnt hair and walking gingerly on the unaccustomed height of a pair of French heels, Tilly made her entrance into the dining room. But of the elegant marquess there was no sign. Her father sat at the head of the long mahogany table, the dappled sunlight from the garden outside playing across his face. His face!

It seemed to have slipped oddly to one side. Tilly stopped and stood very still, her heart beating fast. The room was very quiet. Suddenly a thrush bounced up and down on the branch of a rosebush outside the open window and poured his vital, throbbing spring song into the silence.

"Papa," whispered Tilly. Then louder, "Papa!"

But Lord Charles was dead.

The marquess had declined lunch and had left Lord Charles alone with his debts and his worries. Lord Charles had fretted over the new idea that had he not endured the royal visit, then he would not be in this horrendous financial mess.

He would have to sell Jeebles.

He had looked around the graceful room,

at the silk panels on the walls, cleaned and restored in honor of His Majesty's visit, at the graceful Hepplewhite chairs, and then through the long windows to the calm English vista of lawns and old trees and all the bursting life of spring. The realization of what it would mean to him to lose his family home had struck him like a blow over the heart. He had a massive stroke and died almost instantly, the tired look of pain and loss and bewilderment fading from his eyes.

Tilly stretched out a trembling hand to ring the bell for the butler. After all, one always rang for a servant to sort out one's troubles. But this was one trouble that no retinue of servants could cure.

The Honorable Matilda was now alone in the world.

And penniless.

CHAPTER TWO

" 'Stand back, I tell you, or I may trounce some of you, even as I have him whose carcass, without his head, lies in yonder glade! There, dogs! Take it and glut your eyes with the trunkless head of him who had a stouter heart than any hound among ye!" So saying, he threw the gashed head of Sir Guy into the Baron's arms, who as instantly threw it among his men with a roar of terror, as if it had been a ball of red-hot iron; none of them were more eager than their lord to retain possession of it, and it fell to the ground to be kicked from one to the other.

The sound of carriage wheels outside made Tilly start and she dropped her penny dreadful on the carpet. Lady Aileen was back from her calls! Tilly hurriedly picked up *Robin Hood and Little John; or The Merry Men of Sherwood* and stuffed it under the sofa cushions. She then picked up a copy of *Manners for Women* by Mrs. Humphry, and pretended to read.

With a sigh of relief, Tilly realized that Aileen had gone directly upstairs to her rooms, probably to lie down.

Her hand stole under the cushions to retrieve the penny dreadful, and then stopped. No, it was not the time for escape. It was time to carefully go over this horrible change in her life and try to see how she could make the best of it.

It was a year since her father had died, a long, weary year of watching every bit of her home finally going under the hammer until Jeebles itself, with all its lands, had been sold to a foreign count. Every penny of the sale had gone to pay off Lord Charles's staggering debts, leaving Tilly with a small annuity from the residue of fifty pounds a year; a genteel amount that would suffice if she were prepared to waste her life away in some small boardinghouse full of equally indigent gentlewomer

And then, like an angel from heaven, Lady Aileen had arrived with her parents, the Duke and Duchess of Glenstraith. Lady Aileen had prettily explained their concern for poor Tilly. She, Aileen, was about to embark on her first Season and had come to offer dear Tilly a post as paid companion. "Of course, we will *really* be friends, Tilly," Aileen had explained, and her fond parents had beamed at this superb example of their daughter's magnanimity.

The duke and duchess hardly ever visited their estates in Scotland, preferring their town house in Grosvenor Square, London.

Tilly had been suitably grateful, and in no time at all it seemed her life had changed, but in a singularly unpleasant way, for Aileen's motives had been far from pure. She seemed to enjoy the ridiculous social spectacle presented by her gauche companion and gained herself a small reputation as a wit by describing some of the "Beast's" more gauche remarks. She cleverly built up a new character for the naive and unsophisticated Tilly—that of a bumbling Victorian dragon. "Oh, I couldn't go *there,*" she would explain prettily to her court of young men. "Tilly wouldn't let me."

And poor, unsophisticated Tilly played right into her hands. The glittering youth of social London embarrassed her dreadfully and she was apt to reply to any conversational sally with a grunt. She was unused to wearing skirts and would therefore stride mannishly into a room and flop down on a chair with her legs spread apart.

Tilly's education had been scant, having only had the benefit of a governess for a mere two years of her young life. Her mind was still very immature. She lived in the pages of penny dreadfuls, filling her lonely hours with glorious tales with titles such as *The Jew Detective, The Blue Dwarf,* and the aforementioned *Robin Hood.* She read American imports such as *Unravelling the Twisted Skein; or Deadwood Dick in Gotham,* and *The Ghouls of Galveston,* and she followed the adventures of Frank Reade's *The Steam Man,* a metal steam-driven coal-burning robot, wearing a topper out of which poured smoke as the robot waded into the Comanches.

She vaguely dreamed of marriage to some good sort of fellow with a predilection for hunting. She often thought of the handsome marquess, but only as a man she would like to have as a friend. She was not for one minute aware that she had fallen in love with him during the king's visit. Her comics were no help in educating her mind along the path of passion, for her heroes, if they did get married, seemed to enter into a sort of fourth-form friendship.

She looked around the room, feeling lost and somehow foreign. The Duke and Duchess of Glenstraith were very "up-to-date" as the latest slang had it.

They slavishly followed the Art Nouveau movement and had had all their massive Victorian furniture enameled in dazzling white. Sticky-looking chintzes with large cabbage roses were draped over the sofas and chairs and uncompromisingly hard William Morris settles flanked one of the latest gas fires, a terrifying sort of black-lead sarcophagus hung with asbestos stalactites that glowed red when the gas was lit.

A sort of chandelier embellished with glass flowers hanging on brass stalks hung down from the center of the ceiling, and in the center of each flower was a glass electric light bulb that shed an orange-yellow antiseptic glow, quite unlike the soft light from the old oil lamps back at Jeebles.

I shall have to talk to Aileen, thought Tilly. *I'll ask her not to make fun of me and then maybe she will advise me how to behave.*

Tilly was to accompany Aileen to a ball that night. She had not been told that she must not dance or that she was expected to sit with the chaperones, but in some strange way it seemed to be expected of her.

The gong was rung for afternoon tea and Tilly wearily made her way to the drawing room. Tea was too delicate an affair for Tilly's robust appetite, consisting as it did of tiny cucumber sandwiches, wafer-thin bread, and thin fingers of cake. She longed for one of her old nanny's nursery teas, with bread slices like doorstops and fat slices of plum cake. But nanny was dead, having waited only a month before following her master to the grave.

It had been a source of wonder that Tilly had no relatives to take care of her, but such was the case, both Lord and Lady Charles having hailed from singularly sickly and short-lived families.

The duchess, Aileen's mother, was already presiding over the teapot. There were no guests.

The duchess betrayed her Scottish heritage by being built like a Highland cow. She had a great, lowering, massive face, which was very hairy, and wore large hats that always seemed to have embellishments sticking out of them like horns.

She was dressed in a rose-colored silk blouse with a huge bertha of Irish lace and a long black skirt. For once her hat was a plain biscuit straw, but it was adorned with two huge, bristling steel hatpins that curled up like the horns of the animal she so resembled.

"Sit down, Tilly," she barked. "My fairy's lying down." The fairy was Aileen.

"You should have gone with her today," went on the duchess, pouring tea. "Like to know what she gets up to, and it's not often she don't want you along. Thoughtful gel!"

"Quite," said Tilly faintly. She always found the duchess rather overwhelming. Like most people who have absolutely no manners at all, the duchess felt that she was the one best suited to train her daughter's companion in the social arts.

"Have you read your etiquette book?" she demanded, putting three small cucumber sandwiches into her mouth at once.

"Y-yes," stammered Tilly.

"Where have you got to?"

"The bit about snubbing. 'The woman who cannot snub, on occasion, may be pronounced almost incapable of giving good dinners,' " quoted Tilly dutifully.

"Quite right," said Her Grace. "The world is full of nasty pushing toads who don't know their places. Keep up the good work. Pity no one's come to call, but they must know my fairy's getting a rest before this ball. I've only got you to talk to and it's a bit boring, but nonetheless I'll have to put up with it."

Tea was enlivened by the arrival of the duke. He was a very tall, very thin man with a vague apologetic air, and he aspired to dandyism in a timid way. He was wearing a single-breasted sack suit with the latest in peg-top trousers, a high wing collar, and a polka-dot tie. He was carrying a novel in one hand.

"Found this in the library," he twittered. "Who's been reading this muck?" He brandished a copy of Elinor Glyn's *Vicissitudes of Evangeline,* which had just been published and damned in the press as "scandalous."

"I have," said his lady indifferently, removing a piece of watercress from one of the long hairs on her chin. "Wanted to see what all the fuss was about. There's nothing in it except that it says that the heroine looks very becoming in bed."

"What's up with that?" asked Tilly, forgetting her usual silent role in her surprise.

The duchess looked at her with contempt. "No nice woman wants to look becoming in bed, that's what!"

"I will not have that word spoken in this house!" declared the duke with surprising vigor.

"What word?"

"Bed!"

"Tcha!" said the wife of his bosom nastily. "What do I say to the upstairs maid if she leaves wrinkles in the sheet, eh what? 'Mary, you haven't made the er—er up properly.' She'll think I'm talking about the piss-pot."

The duke subsided, yet looked ready to cry at this final vulgarity. Tilly took pity on him and tried to change the conversation. "What's the country like at Glenstraith?" she asked. "Good hunting?"

"Don't know," said the duke. "Cruel sport. Poor little foxes."

Tilly felt flushed and crushed. She had never thought of foxes as anything other than vermin. It seemed as if every single one of her ideas was wrong in this strange city.

"The Marquess of Heppleford hunts," she finally said.

"Heppleford?" said the duke, momentarily diverted. "Sound chap. Something funny about his old man's will, you know. His father died not long before yours and, of course, he inherited the title, but there wasn't a will. Now the will's turned up in one of the books in the library and Heppleford's gone to see his lawyers today. He'll be at the Quennell's ball tonight but—I mean—there shouldn't be any difficulty. He'll inherit all right. The old marquess didn't have any other heirs to speak of. He's a rich young man in his own right, of course."

Tilly felt suddenly elated at the thought of seeing the marquess again. Perhaps he might even ask her for a dance. . . .

Poor Tilly had been dubbed the "Beast" by Lady Aileen and her frivolous friends. The Marquess of Heppleford, on the other hand, had long enjoyed the title of "Beauty." Because of his startling good looks, he enjoyed high popularity with both sexes, the men accounting him no end of a good fellow and the ladies, down to the last crusty dowager, swooning at his approach. He had remained remarkably unspoiled by all this adulation, having a cynical turn of mind combined with a sunny good nature.

At that moment, however, he looked neither beautiful nor good-natured. His perfect features were marred by an angry scowl as he allowed his valet to assist him into a boiled shirt. His father had been very strange indeed before his death. He had frequently preached to his son on the merits of married bliss, aided and abetted by the marquess's two aunts, who had marriageable daughters.

Now the late marquess's will had descended on his heir like a bombshell. The marquess naturally inherited the title, but he would not see one penny of his father's considerable personal fortune were he not married one month after the reading of the will.

He had planned to marry eventually in his own good time. Now he was forced into a scrambled courtship. Although he was a wealthy young man in his own right, he would need every penny of his father's fortune to keep the family home, Chennington, and estates in good and profitable order.

One aunt, Lady Mary Swingleton, had three daughters and the other, Lady Bertha Anderson, had two. All were quite well-favored girls, but the marquess had no intention of marrying one of his second cousins just to oblige. In fact, he was already hell-bent on marrying any girl who would drive his scheming aunts into an apoplexy. He thought briefly of the beautiful Lady Aileen. Now, there was a young miss who would take the shine out of any other aspiring marchioness. Well, he would make haste to further his acquaintance with the beautiful Aileen at the ball that very evening.

Feeling better now that he had decided on at least some vague plan of action, he slowly descended the staircase of his town house in St. James's Square to find his friend Toby Bassett waiting for him in the library.

Toby was often compared to the poet Byron, having a dark and brooding sort of beauty. Like his friend the marquess, he was tall. He had a luxuriant mop of black curls and dark liquid eyes that were often half-hidden by heavy lids. The marquess was well aware that his friend's brooding air of mystery was because Toby was almost always slightly inebriated, being not quite drunk, not quite sober. But the ladies were not so aware, and wove fantastic fantasies to account for Toby's strange, slumbering gaze.

"How did the reading of the will go?" asked Toby indolently from the depths of a Thonet rocking chair.

The marquess briefly outlined the terms.

A look of unholy amusement enlivened Toby's brooding good looks. "Famous," he said. "Nice to see you embroiled in some human difficulties for once, Philip. Had it too easy all your life. Drifted through your exams as a boy, drifted into wealth, drifted into the title . . ."

"It doesn't disturb me now," said the marquess lightly. "I shall drift into marriage just as easily. And who is going to refuse my title or fortune? I was pretty angry at first, and I'd still like to get back at those old tabbies of aunts of mine. I know they made Father put that ridiculous clause in his will."

Toby abruptly lost interest, two minutes being his normal attention span. "Who's the Beast?" he asked. "Glenstraith's girl keeps telling funny stories about her Beast."

"I don't know," said the marquess. "Probably someone she met at one of those society parties. You know, the latest thing. A mad artist or a tattooed boxer or something like that."

"Probably," echoed Toby, adjusting his tie in the looking glass and pulling down his white piqué waistcoat. "Shall we go?"

Tilly turned around in front of the long glass in her bedroom and considered that she looked as well as could be expected. The duchess had insisted on furnishing her with a new ball gown. It seemed very grand to Tilly, who did not know that the duchess had bought it at the Indigent Gentlewoman's Annual Sale for a very small sum indeed, and only then because she was on the committee and felt obliged to buy *something*. Unlike Lady Aileen, who enjoyed the services of a French lady's maid, Tilly had to rely on her own resources. So there was no one around to tell her that the dress was quite unsuitable for a plump red-headed virgin. The dress was made of coral velvet with a blue chiffon fichu that was tied with a black velvet bow at the back. The coral velvet, which clashed quite dreadfully with her red hair, was elaborately embroidered with pink roses and ended in a thick hem of fox fur.

Having decided that her gown, at least, was elegant, Tilly plumped herself down at the dressing table and studied her healthy, tanned complexion in dismay. Since she had been given one of the guest bedrooms, there was an ample supply of unguents and lotions in front of her. "May as well do it properly," muttered Tilly to herself and unscrewed a pot of white enamel that was the foundation base used by every lady from Queen Alexandria down. With a liberal hand, she began to apply it to her face until a white mask stared back at her. Much encouraged, she opened up the onyx powder bowl and liberally applied pearl powder—made from bismuth oxychloride—to her face with a large swansdown puff. Then she tried to blend rouge into her cheeks so that she would have the perfect fashionable doll's face. She had put her hair up over pads so that it seemed at least a foot high. Tilly decided to frizzle her hair at the front with the curling tongs to complete her appearance.

She set the tongs on their little spirit heater and then spat on them to make sure they were hot enough. She raised the tongs to her hair.

"Mademoiselle!" came a sharp cry from the doorway.

Tilly swung around with the curling tongs in her hand to see Aileen's pert French maid, Francine, standing with her hands raised in horror.

"What's the matter?" asked Tilly. "Is anything up with Lady Aileen?"

"No, it is *you,* mademoiselle," said Francine. "The maquillage is so bad for you. All that white. It is bad cosmetic."

Tilly looked at her in surprise and then picked up the jar of enamel. "Seems all right," she said. "It's called Blanc d'Argent. Very pretty."

"But these creams have a base of lead, mademoiselle," said Francine earnestly. "The lead, it eats away at the skin. Even your Jersey Lily, Lillie Langtry, she now have the dreadful skin from such stuff, so. And you must not frizz the hair. You have a natural curl. You have—"

"Francine!" said Lady Aileen, tripping into the room. "You must not stand here gossiping and neglecting your duties."

"I was just telling mademoiselle that the maquillage, it is wrong for her."

"Nonsense," said Aileen. "Let me look at you, Tilly. Why, I never saw you look so grand. You're magnificent. Leave her alone, Francine, and run along, do. Honestly, Tilly," she went on as the maid reluctantly left the room. "You look grand!"

Tilly was surprised and gratified to see actual tears of emotion in Aileen's eyes. She did not know that Aileen was trying to suffocate a delighted burst of giggles. The Beast had surpassed herself. She was too, too utterly marvelous. Just like a clown!

"You look marvelous yourself, Aileen," said Tilly warmly. Aileen did indeed look like an ethereal vision. Her dress was of delicate layers of chiffon in sweet-pea colors and she carried an enormous ostrich-feather fan with diamond-studded sticks.

Despite the unexpected warmth of the evening outside, Tilly was happy and excited when she climbed into the Glenstraith's victoria, which was to convey them to the ball at the Quennell's mansion in Kensington. The victoria lurched dangerously like a ship on a stormy sea as Lady Glenstraith heaved her great hairy bulk into the carriage. Then they were off.

The London Season had begun. From house after house the music of the eternal waltz sounded out into the pale-blue evening —"After the ball is over, after the dance is done . . ."—as they trotted past other carriages with their ladies wearing high head-dresses and their gentlemen in white waistcoats. Soon they were joining the other traffic under the yellow lights of Marble Arch.

Lady Glenstraith was leaning forward to say something to her husband, so Tilly took the opportunity to whisper, "Aileen. I'm so looking forward to this ball. Please . . . oh, please don't make fun of me!"

Aileen's beautiful eyes opened wide. "Make fun of you, my dear Beast? I *never* do. But you must call me 'Lady Aileen' when we are in company, you know."

"And you must call me 'Tilly,' " pleaded Tilly, still in that urgent whisper, "and not Beast."

"Oh, *that!*" was all Aileen would say, shrugging a pretty shoulder.

Tilly sat back in the carriage and bit her lip. She had a sudden aching longing for the freedom of her days at Jeebles. Her evening gown already felt unseasonably warm and her skin itched under its layers upon layers of undergarments.

She miserably reflected that her duties as companion to Lady Aileen were indeed light compared to the lot of other paid companions. She did not need to read books or magazines to her mistress, nor had she a dog to walk. But in some cruel way her presence was always expected, as if Aileen were in need of a perpetual clown. It was an age in which society delighted in jokes, usually at some poor person's expense.

Minor poets, boxers, jockeys, wrestlers, and mediums all found themselves raised to the glittering levels of court circles in order to be prodded and stared at and laughed at, and then just as suddenly, to be dropped back into oblivion.

And poor Tilly blundered about this society like some great immature moth perpetually burning its wings against the glittering flames of the wit of the top ten thousand.

The heavy scent of lime from the trees in the Kensington gardens reminded Tilly of the green oasis that had been Jeebles.

The carriage lurched to a stop outside a great square white mansion. The blinds were drawn and shadows waltzed across them, dipping and swaying.

As Tilly mounted the red carpeted stairs to the ballroom, she began to feel her first twinge of unease, her first inkling that all was not well with her appearance.

The Quennell's debutante daughter, who was waiting at the top of the stairs to receive the guests with her parents, Mr. and Mrs. Jeffrey Quennell, was attired in the same soft pastels as Aileen. One look into the ballroom after she had made her curtsy was enough to confirm Tilly's worst fears. All the young girls of her own age were attired in pink or white or a soft mixture of pale pastel colors. Their faces were free of paint and most had only used *papier poudre* to take the shine from their noses.

Despite long windows opening onto a terrace at the opposite end, the ballroom was uncomfortably warm and Tilly stared down miserably at the fox fur edging her gown and knew, with a sinking feeling, that she had done it again. She was wearing the wrong gown and looked like a freak. Without any prompting she took her place with the chaperons against the wall and miserably hung her head. Someone once said that there is no emotional growth without pain, and in that first painful hour against the wall, watching the glittering, chattering dancers, a little of the gauche, overgrown schoolgirl that was Tilly began to disappear. It was with a young woman's eyes that she glanced across the room in time to see the entrance of the Marquess of Heppleford.

Her heart began to beat uncomfortably against her ribs and something seemed to have happened to her breathing. His hair shone like polished gold in the gaslight of the ballroom and his evening dress was tailored to swooning point.

She suffered her first pangs of envy as she watched him walk quickly to Aileen's side and begin to scribble his name in her little dance card.

Tilly watched the marquess and Aileen performing the lancers and tried to imagine herself in Aileen's place. After the dance finished, the gentlemen were allowed to walk with their partners until the next one was announced. It was a marvelous opportunity, as even Tilly knew, for unchaperoned flirtation, and the marquess walked with Lady Aileen straight through the long windows and out onto the terrace and down the marble steps into the gardens. Tilly's heart sank. Her heroes of the comics had no answer to this situation. What would Deadwood Dick or Jack Harkaway do in a situation like this?

The marquess, who had planned to further his acquaintance with the enchanting Lady Aileen, was annoyed to find that the garden was already full of groups of young people enjoying the warm night air. He was just about to compliment Aileen neatly on her appearance when the couple were accosted by a noisy group of young men and women. "How's your Beast?" cried one. "She looks a regular guy tonight and oh, my stars, that dress!"

"Dragonish as ever," said Aileen, smiling. "I am sure she will pursue me any minute to find out what I am doing in the moonlight. I am sure my Beast thinks that moonlight is such a lot of *rot.*"

Her audience laughed appreciatively with the exception of the marquess. "Who is this Beast?" he asked.

Aileen waved her long ostrich-feather fan languidly back and forth. "Oh, it's my companion, poor Tilly Burningham. She's called the Beast because she's too frightful-looking for words. She follows me around like a dog, and if I'm not too terribly careful, she's apt to slap me on the back and call me a *jolly good fellow.*"

"You're wicked!" shrieked a girl with an admiring look. "Hasn't the Beast got any feelings?"

"I suppose so," said Aileen, enjoying her audience. "Who knows what passions lurk in the Beast's bosom. Do you know she actually reads all those penny dreadfuls? If you look under the sofa cushions in our house, it's simply *stuffed* with them. Oh, my dear Lord Philip, how you scowl! You must think me very cruel to my poor Beast."

"Yes," said the marquess. "Isn't Tilly Lord Charles's girl? Is she a guest of yours?"

"No, no!" cried Aileen, all mock horror. "Tilly is my *paid* companion. And very well paid she is too."

"Your next partner will be waiting for you," said the marquess, listening to the opening chords of a quadrille.

Lady Aileen moved very close to him. She was wearing a perfume called Jordan Water, bought at ten guineas a flask at Madame Rachel's beauty salon in Bond Street, and she wanted to make sure he received the full benefit of it. Visions of being married and a marchioness, and all at the beginning of her first Season, danced before Aileen's eyes. "I shall look forward to our next dance then . . . Philip," she breathed in the husky accents of her favorite actress and then, with what she believed was a *killing,* seductive movement, she drew the feathers of her ostrich fan across the marquess's face.

He looked down at her with a slightly stunned expression on his face at her effrontery, but Aileen thought Cupid's arrow had pierced his heart and went off with her next partner, well-satisfied.

Having no partner for the next dance himself, the marquess went off in search of the bar and found his friend, Toby, drinking champagne with single-minded absorption.

"Found a wife yet?" asked Toby, his heavy-lidded eyes looking sleepier than ever. "Saw you mooning off with the Glenstraith chit."

"Little tart," said the marquess succinctly, helping himself to champagne. "Spends all her time mocking that lumpy companion of hers."

"Doesn't make her a tart," commented Toby, fairly.

"No, but she called me Philip and wiped that bloody fan of hers across my face."

"Oh, I say, that's going a bit far," said

Toby, showing rare animation. "Well, there's lots of other girls."

"I'm tired of the whole thing," said the marquess. "I think I'll go and give the Beast a dance."

"Which beast?"

"Tilly Burningham. Aileen's companion."

Tilly had reached that hypersensitive wallflower state where she felt the eye of everyone in the room was on her. She ached to be allowed to go home, to scrub the makeup from her face, and to indulge in a hearty cry. Tilly had not cried for a long time, not even after the death of her father. There had been too much to do, what with the funeral to arrange and then the exhausting months of winding up her father's convoluted and bankrupt affairs.

To her horror, she felt the treacherous prick of tears behind her eyelids and was concentrating so much on pulling herself together that it was a few minutes before she realized that the marquess was standing in front of her and that he had said something.

"May I have this dance, Miss Burningham?" he said again. Tilly rose awkwardly to her feet. She did not offer him her dance card, since it was empty of names. Feeling as if she had been raised from the depths of misery into some warm and delicious dream, Tilly mutely allowed herself to be borne off into the steps of a waltz, gloved hand holding gloved hand. Tilly was an awkward dancer, moving clumsily on her high heels, and the marquess found he had to be extra nimble on his feet to avoid being trodden on. He did not bother to talk, feeling he had done enough in asking her to dance and, as for Tilly, she was too overcome by the thrill of being held in this magnificent man's arms to open her mouth.

"Beauty and the Beast!" said Aileen, giggling, as she floated past in the arms of her partner. Tilly did not hear her but the marquess did and he steered Tilly as far away from Aileen as possible.

Somewhat to his annoyance he found it was the supper dance and led the bemused Tilly toward the long room where refreshments were being served. Tilly felt as if she were being led into some magic palace. Each table had its lamp with a canopy of tight red silk, its pale, plump quail, its mountain of strawberries, and its bowl of gardenias floating in their own private arctic of ice.

"Are you enjoying the dance, Miss Burningham?" asked the marquess politely.

"Oh, yes, awfully . . . awfully jolly, I mean,"

said Tilly. "I mean ripping people and all that."

"Quite," said the marquess, privately wondering how soon he could make his escape. "I was distressed to learn of your father's death."

"Well, it *was* rather awful," said Tilly, suddenly and embarrassingly conscious of the interested stares being directed at their table. "I mean, having to sell up as well. But I'm lucky to have a job."

"It's an unusual job for so young a girl," said the marquess.

"I s'pose so," said Tilly. "But Aileen's a jolly sort of girl. Absolutely ripping," said Tilly, resolutely banishing other nastier thoughts of Aileen to the back of her mind. After all, if it weren't for Aileen, then she wouldn't be sitting here talking away to the catch of the London Season!

"So," went on the marquess, neatly dissecting a quail with the precision of a surgeon, "you must be enjoying your life in London. All the balls and parties."

"I miss Jeebles, you know," began Tilly. "Oh . . . rats!"

She had been trying to copy the marquess's dexterity with her knife and fork but the treacherous quail skidded wildly and landed on the floor.

"Leave it," said the marquess, trying to block out the delighted giggles of Aileen and her court. A liveried footman appeared suddenly and deftly slid another bird under Tilly's blushing face. She looked at it miserably.

"Go on," said the marquess gently. He was suddenly reminded of a time when he had had to entertain a friend's schoolboy son to dinner. "Jeebles. You were saying how much you missed it."

"Yes, I suppose I'm a country girl at heart. Jolly ripping in the country," said poor Tilly, suddenly amazed at her own lack of vocabulary, her inability to find the right words to conjure up a picture of all her beloved home had meant to her. *Any minute now,* thought the marquess, *she's going to say, "Yes, sir, please sir," just like a schoolboy.*

"Doesn't the duchess find it odd that her daughter should want such a young companion?" he asked. "And you are not eating anything."

"I shall in a minute," said Tilly. "No, Aileen—I mean, Lady Aileen—told her parents she was doing it as a sort of favor cos I didn't have any money."

"Has the duchess given you any duties?"

Tilly looked at him in innocent surprise. "No, I mean, why should she? I'm Lady Aileen's companion."

"She will," said the marquess dryly and then could have bitten off his tongue, because Tilly was looking at him in bewildered amazement. Aileen would soon tire of her Beast, he thought, and the duchess would take Tilly over and then this odd, awkward girl would find that her life consisted of trotting around after the formidable duchess to endless committee meetings.

"I have troubles of my own," he said lightly to change the subject. "My father's will has just been found, and under the terms of it, I find I must marry in a month's time."

"Oh, how simply *awful!*" said Tilly, suddenly breathless and nervous. "I mean, what if, because you're in such a rush, you end up married to someone you don't like?"

"It could happen," said the marquess, thinking of Aileen. Had she not revealed herself to be such a shallow miss, he could have well proposed!

"What type of man would you like to get married to, Miss Burningham?" he asked in a light, teasing voice that sent delicious shivers down Tilly's well-corseted spine.

"Oh, I don't know," she said, staring at her

still untouched food. "Someone to hunt with, be friends with, well . . . some good sort, you know." She gave an awkward laugh and drank a glass of wine as if it were lemonade.

"But then, you would become just another kind of companion," said the marquess, gently taking Tilly's plate and beginning to dissect the quail in the way a mother cuts food up into small pieces for her child.

"No, *really,*" said Tilly desperately. He didn't know who to marry! Could he be considering her? "I would have my own home, maybe somewhere like Jeebles and . . . and . . . I wouldn't bother him much."

"I have a place like Jeebles," said the marquess slowly.

Tilly looked across the little table at him, wide-eyed, and the marquess stared back.

He wondered if it were a trick of the light, but he suddenly seemed to be seeing two girls: one the awkward, badly dressed schoolgirl, and superimposed over it, for the minute, a wide-blue-eyed, innocent, very feminine girl. Then Tilly crinkled up her eyes and gave a jolly laugh to hide her embarrassment and the illusion was gone.

"It doesn't *look* like Jeebles," he went on. "It's all medieval battlements outside and Eighteenth Century rococo inside. But I've got a one thousand-acre estate with all the sorts of things you had at Jeebles—park and farms and that sort of thing."

"Your wife would have to know how to get on with the tenants," said Tilly, forgetting her awkwardness. "I mean, it's very important to visit them and look after them and all that." She suddenly blushed as she remembered the overheard conversation of Mrs. Pomfret, the lodge keeper's wife.

"Oh, I don't know that that side of it's all that important," said the marquess. "I have a damn good manager and, believe me, tenants would rather have someone who looked after the *practical* side of things, like repairing roofs and fences and so on, than some nosy Lady Bountiful dropping in at awkward times with chicken soup."

They would indeed, thought Tilly sadly, but there was no one to tell her. She applied herself to her food and the marquess leaned back in his chair, watching her from under half-closed eyelids and wondering what he had said to upset her. And why on earth had he told this odd girl about his marriage plans? Imagine if he were to be wed to *her*. How shocked and disappointed his aunts would be! The thought of how shocked and disappointed they would be suddenly appealed immensely to him and he studied Tilly with new eyes.

She hadn't looked that bad, he reflected, in her riding clothes. It was all that paint on her face and that dreadful dress that made her look such a fright. Now, just suppose he *did* marry this girl, he would be supplying her with a home, he would gain an undemanding wife who knew how to run a mansion, and he would infuriate his relatives into the bargain.

"Where's my Beast?" cried a light, tinkling voice. Aileen was bending over Tilly's shoulder, pressing her glowing, beautiful face next to Tilly's own, showing the marquess what a contrast they made.

The marquess found he was actually beginning to dislike Aileen immensely. He would love to see Aileen's face if he wed Tilly. But, oh, Tilly! She was looking nervous and miserable and guilty, as if she sensed that under Aileen's laughter her mistress was not pleased that dowdy Tilly had kept this handsome lord away from the ballroom for so long.

"Have you forgotten, *dear* Lord Philip," said Aileen, smiling, "that we have a dance?" She waved her little program in front of his nose.

"As a matter of fact, I have," said the marquess, knowing he was being rude but enjoying the look of stunned surprise on Aileen's pretty face. "Are you ready Miss Burningham? Come, Lady Aileen, we shall escort Miss Burningham back to the ballroom and then we shall dance."

Relegated again to the row of chaperons, Tilly watched the marquess and Aileen dance past. She gave a little sigh. All she could do was treasure this evening up against the dreary, humiliating days to come; this evening when he had talked to her and looked at her and danced with her.

Tilly no longer wanted the marquess as a friend. She wanted him as a lover. But she did not yet know it and could only wonder why the sight of Aileen in the marquess's well-tailored arms should distress her so much.

To her amazement, Tilly became aware that she was being confronted by yet another handsome man. "May I introduce myself?" said this vision in a drawling voice. "I'm a friend of Heppleford's. Toby Bassett at your service. Dance, Miss Burningham?"

Toby had drunk himself slightly sober. He had had a sudden impulse to dance but did not know who to ask. He was too lazy to begin to solicit all the pretty girls only to find at this late stage of the ball that all their dance cards were full. His friend Philip had seemed to be entertained enough with Miss Burningham; therefore, he had decided to ask Tilly.

He danced solemnly around and around on the same spot until the waves of wine began to encompass him again and he began to reel slightly. He hardly ever danced and he slowly began to remember why. It was because he always fell down.

"I am very drunk, Miss Burningham," he said, performing a graceful turn and scrunching down on one of Tilly's feet.

Tilly was used to very drunk men from her days on the hunting field and found nothing amiss. She only considered him very much a gentleman to tell her so.

"Perhaps we could go out into the garden?" she suggested. "The night air might clear your head."

"Splendid idea," he said amiably, holding tightly onto her gloved arm for support. "Lead the way!"

Feeling more comfortable than she had done all evening, Tilly propelled him through the long windows and helped him to negotiate the steps.

Behind them in the ballroom the stunned eyes of Lady Aileen and the Marquess of Heppleford watched them go.

"Now, just sit down here," Tilly was saying, guiding him to a rustic bench. A large pale moon stared down on the garden and a light, balmy breeze sent the shadows of the leaves dancing on the silver grass. The garden was empty apart from themselves and Tilly gave a sigh of relief and leaned back and closed her eyes, imagining herself back in the peace and quiet of the country.

A gentle snore from her companion made her open her eyes and turn around. Toby Bassett had fallen asleep, his head resting on his chest and his gloved hands neatly folded in his lap. He would be better for his sleep, thought Tilly, feeling maternal. The leaves and flowers rustled in the night wind and the jaunty sound of a polka echoed faintly from the ballroom upstairs. Tilly was content to sit silently beside the sleeping Toby, glad to be away from the hard stares and heat of the ballroom.

Lady Aileen thought the polka would never come to an end. First Tilly Burningham had taken the marquess off to the supper room and now she was flirting with that gorgeously handsome Toby Bassett—walking off with him into the garden without so much as a by-your-leave. The polka at last swung to a noisy close and Aileen's partner joined the rest in crying for an encore. To Aileen's dismay, the band struck up again and she was pulled back into the dance.

The Marquess of Heppleford was also wondering what on earth had happened to Toby and Tilly. Toby rarely danced, and drunk or sober or in between, he was never in the habit of squiring young ladies in the moonlight. And Tilly Burningham of all people. But hadn't he himself found her rather endearing in an odd way? The dance at last came to a close and Aileen, followed by her court of admirers, hurried down the stairs into the garden. Unfortunately for Tilly, Toby had, but a moment before, come awake and had been overwhelmed with gratitude that this young female whose name he had forgotten had let him sleep undisturbed. Just as Aileen was descending the stairs he was saying, "You know, you're a very good sort of girl," and he followed it up with an affectionate kiss on Tilly's cheek.

"Miss Burningham!" exclaimed Aileen, forgetting her usual silvery tones in her wrath. "You appear to forget that you are employed by me as a companion. Back to the ballroom *immediately.*"

"Of course, Aileen—I mean *Lady* Aileen," said Tilly, jumping to her feet.

"Allow me to escort you," said Toby, rising languidly and staring down at Tilly with those brooding eyes that made all the watching female's hearts beat faster.

"That will not be necessary," said Aileen. "Come, Tilly."

And Tilly went, head bent, listening to an acid lecture on her *forwardness*, her impertinence, her lack of duty.

"Aileen's *jealous* of her Beast," cried a girl from the garden with a maddening giggle. Aileen heard the remark and vowed that something must be done with the infuriating Tilly to put her in her place and keep her there.

Tilly regained her former seat among the staring, whispering chaperons and bent her head. She felt very tired.

Slightly flushed, Aileen was claimed by her next partner. Dance followed dance, hour followed hour. Would the ball never end?

But at long last they were all in the victoria again, bowling homeward. A gray, pearly dawn was rising over London and thin, ghostlike wreaths of mist hung in the branches of the trees in Hyde Park. The scavengers were out sluicing the pavements, which turned from gray to watery blue as the rising sun burned away the mist. Somewhere a blackbird sang an ecstatic song to the new day as the carriages of the rich rolled on, bearing their burden of jaded faces homeward. Aileen's mouth was folded into a thin line. She had not yet had a chance to tell her mother of Tilly's disgraceful behavior.

Perhaps, after all, Aileen might not have complained to her mother about Tilly, since she was of too shallow a nature to sustain any emotion for long, be it love or anger, but the duchess opened her great hairy mouth as the carriage rolled along under the trees to remind her daughter of the startling information that Heppleford would have to get married to someone—anyone—before the month were up, or he would not inherit.

Aileen remembered the marquess's strange interest in Tilly. Good Heavens! Perhaps he meant to marry Tilly and that would *never* do. She, Aileen, would be made a laughing stock if her Beast were to go to the altar first—and with the handsomest man in London!

Accordingly, as soon as the victoria had rolled to a stop in front of the duchess's town house, Aileen asked "Mumsie" to trot along to her bedroom for "a little chat."

The duchess was much gratified. Her

daughter hardly ever seemed to want her company these days.

She listened in amazement to the tale of Tilly's forwardness.

"I felt it was wrong of you to have such a *young* girl as a companion," said the duchess, shifting her great bulk around on the end of Aileen's bed and trying to make herself comfortable. "That girl, Tilly, needs a firm hand. And those balls and parties have gone to her head. You've been too soft with her, my puss. I'll take her over. She can help me with my committees. That'll instill into her a sense of gratitude. Don't worry your sweet head, pet. Let Mumsie see to everything."

Aileen stretched and yawned and pouted and wished her mother would go away now that Tilly was going to be taken care of, but her mother was still mulling over the news about the Marquess of Heppleford.

"Do you think he'll propose to you, Aileen?" she asked anxiously.

"I'm sure he would if I encouraged him," said Aileen, yawning.

The duchess drew her brows together in massive thought. "A little dinner, I think, my poppet. We'll invite him for next week. And it will be good for him to see Tilly in her proper place, you know. After all, she *is* only a sort of glorified servant. . . ."

But Aileen had fallen asleep, serene and content as only a very beautiful debutante with rich and powerful parents could be.

CHAPTER THREE

"Miss Stapleton will read the minutes of the last meeting," intoned the duchess. "Hand me my reading spectacles, Tilly."

Tilly complied and settled back in her hard chair to endure yet another of the duchess's committees. "Don't *slouch,*" hissed the duchess, and Tilly jerked her spine bolt upright. The duchess had taken to strapping Tilly into a backboard for two hours each day to "stiffen her spine." And, as if the mahogany slab were not enough agony, a violin string was tied around Tilly's shoulders so that it cut painfully into her flesh if she so much as moved an inch.

The Taking Over of Tilly had started the day after the ball and Tilly tossed and turned at night, tortured by dreams in which the duchess's great, hairy, disembodied face mouthed, "Don't slouch!" over and over again.

The committee meeting was taking place in the boardroom of a home for Disreputable Women. The duchess and her equally militant companions would often drive about the streets in search of disreputable women and, having found them, thrust them triumphantly into a home. Several members of the Fallen were lined up against one wall, eyeing their tormentors sullenly.

Miss Stapleton droned on with the minutes and Tilly reviewed the events of the past week. Gone were the balls and picnics and parties. Instead she had to read to the duchess, massage the duchess's muscular shoulders, and follow her to committee meetings, carrying all the duchess's paraphernalia of patent medicines, improving tracts, and reading glasses in her reticule.

Tilly's face, scrubbed free of makeup, shone in the warm, musty air of the boardroom. Her hair was scraped back into a bun at the nape of her neck and she wore a hot serge skirt, a striped blouse with a hard celluloid collar and tie, and a straw boater, all of which the duchess considered suitable wear. Tilly's only pleasure was in eating, each large meal with its attendent glasses of wine serving to dull the humiliation of her existence. She no longer found any enjoyment in the penny dreadfuls and had taken to reading romantic novels, substituting, in her imagination, the marquess for the hero. She had daydreamed so intensely about him since the night of the ball that it was almost a shock to hear the duchess discussing him over the tea and biscuits after the meeting.

"Heppleford's coming for dinner," she told her cronies. "Great hopes there. You know, of course, that he's got to get married?"

"Of course," echoed Lady Wayne, a tall, angular committee member. "How did you manage it? We've *all* invited him to dinner and he's refused every single invitation. He won't even look at those cousins of his."

"My fairy is very beautiful," said the duchess in a smug voice.

Lady Wayne bridled. "My little Emily is accounted quite a picture. Perhaps there is some other attraction. . . ." she added maliciously with a sly look in Tilly's direction. She lowered her voice to a sort of booming whisper. "He spent quite a bit of time with her at the Quennell ball, you know."

"Nothing to it," replied the duchess with a

massive sneer. "He knew her father. Taking pity on her, mark my words."

Tilly heard the last words and came down from her dreamworld with a bump. She had been indulging in a glorious vision of the dinner party, where the handsome marquess had eyes for no one but herself.

She was relieved when the duchess suddenly produced a turnip of a watch and exclaimed it was time to leave.

She climbed into the victoria after the duchess and sat with her back to the horses. The hard sparkle of the sun hurt her eyes. It bounced from the white, fluttering blinds of the shops, from the plate glass of the windows and glittered on the burnished roofs. The press of horse traffic was immense and hot smells of manure mingled with the smell of dust. A pieman jogged past, his tray of steaming pies on a level with Tilly's nose. All London was hot and baking. Flushed faces wilted above boned and celluloid collars. The duchess's great red, hairy face seemed to burn like a Highland sunset and the sunlight glittered and flashed on her huge steel hatpins. Above the burning city stretched a sky of deep, fierce blue—*Like Philip's eyes*, thought Tilly with a sudden stab of pain. She wanted to cherish and nurse her dreams. She did not want to be faced with the reality of his presence that evening. She was so absorbed in this novel thought that it was a few seconds before she realized the carriage had stopped and the duchess was barking at her from the pavement "to stop gawking and dreaming."

The Glenstraith's house was musty and cool behind drawn blinds, the servants moving quietly through its subterranean light. Tilly longed to stretch out on her bed after releasing her body from its prison of stays and her swollen ankles from the torture of a pair of high buttoned boots. But no sooner had she removed her straw hat when she was summoned again to the duchess's presence.

The Duchess of Glenstraith was in her bedroom. As Tilly entered, Her Grace was just in the act of plonking her great hairy feet into a basin of cold water. *So,* thought Tilly unromantically, *must the Highland cow cool his hot hooves in the chill waters of a Highland bog*.

"Read to me," ordered the duchess. "You'll find *The Times* over there. Read the letters."

Tilly stifled a sigh. A barrel organ was playing "My Little Grey Home in the West" somewhere at the end of the street, the tinny music rendered poignant by distance. And

71

the unbearably hot world of the outdoors seemed infinitely desirable now that it was shut away behind a screen of thick lace-edged blinds.

Tilly read mindlessly and then suddenly concentrated on what she was reading as the writer's ironic humor penetrated her tired brain. The writer to the *The Times* was complaining that although the opera management of Covent Garden regulated the dress of its male patrons, it did not do the same for the females. The writer explained that he had worn the regulation evening dress. Tilly read:

> "I wore the costume imposed on me by the regulations of the house. Evening dress is cheap, simple, durable, and prevents rivalry and extravagance on the part of male leaders of fashion, annihilates class distinctions, and gives men who are poor and doubtful of their social position (that is, the great majority of men) a sense of security and satisfaction that no clothes of their own choosing could confer, besides saving a whole sex the trouble of considering what they should wear on state occasions. . . .

But I submit that what is sauce for the goose is sauce for the gander. . . .

At nine o'clock (the opera began at eight) a lady came in and sat down very conspicuously in my line of sight. She remained there until the beginning of the last act. I do not complain of her coming late and going early; on the contrary, I wish she had come later and gone earlier. For this lady, who had very black hair, had stuck over her right ear the pitiable corpse of a large white bird, which looked exactly as if someone had killed it by stamping on its breast and then nailing it to the lady's temple, which was presumably of sufficient solidity to bear the operation. I am not, I hope, a morbidly squeamish person, but the spectacle sickened me. I presume that if I had presented myself at the doors with a dead snake round my neck, a collection of blackbeetles pinned to my shirtfront, and a grouse in my hair, I should have been refused admission."

Tilly looked up, her eyes crinkling with laughter, and then stared in dismay at the look of purple rage on the duchess's face.

"Who wrote that—that *twaddle*," spluttered Her Grace.

Tilly peered at the signature in the gloom of the bedroom. "Someone called G. Bernard Shaw," she said.

"Might have known," said the duchess, her agitated feet sending a great slop of water over the side of the basin. "Troublemaker!"

Tilly remembered with much amusement that the duchess herself possessed such a hat.

But the duchess's next remark wiped the amusement from her face.

"I say, Tilly," said Her Grace, lifting one foot out of the water and staring in seeming wonder at her toes, which well she might, since they looked like globe artichokes, "there's no need for you to attend this dinner tonight. Be happier with a tray in your room, what? You never like this social twaddle anyway."

Tilly felt suddenly rebellious. "I would like very much to attend," she said in a choked voice.

"Well, you ain't going to, so there," said Her Grace nastily.

Tilly gave a stifled sound and fled from the room. She reached the sanctuary of her bedroom and hurled herself onto the bed and cried and cried. Now that there was no possibility of seeing the marquess, her fickle heart told her that that was what she really wanted more than anything in the world. Her dreams and fantasies could no longer sustain her. She cried for the fall of the Burninghams, for the death of her father, for the humiliating days of her present existence. She cried so long and so heartily that it was some time before she became aware that someone was pressing a cool handkerchief soaked in cologne against her hot forehead. She twisted around and looked up into the sympathetic eyes of Francine. "You must not cry, mademoiselle," said the lady's maid softly. "I shall make you some tea and you will feel better. I, Francine, shall be upstairs also this evening, so we shall play the cards and I shall tell you very, *very* scandalous stories."

"You're dashed decent, Francine," said Tilly, sobbing. "A real brick."

Francine said nothing and simply took Tilly's hot little hand in her own and sat quietly at the edge of the bed until the girl's sobs had ceased.

They made an odd contrast, the flushed, tousled, and tearful Tilly and the cool and svelte lady's maid with her neat black hair and snapping black eyes. But it was the beginning of a real friendship, a friendship that

75

was to mean more to Tilly than she could ever begin to guess.

The marquess shifted uneasily in his chair later that day and wished he had not come. The heat in the dining room was oppressive. Various Art Nouveau products of Louis Comfort Tiffany winked at him from the table and a madonna by Edvard Munch seemed to waver restlessly on the wall. The baking heat of the outside walls of the house had finally penetrated to the interior. Flowers wilted sadly in their bowls of melted ice.

Philip had hoped to see that strange tomboyish girl again, since he felt sorry for her, but she was unaccountably absent. The heavy meal and heavy wine combined with the heat of the room made him feel sleepy, and he would have been content to relax and exchange desultory pieces of conversation with the duke had it not been for Lady Aileen, who restlessly sparkled at him and postured and tittered and chattered. Any time she looked like flagging before the almost tangible air of boredom emanating from the marquess, her mother would spur her to fresh efforts with great nudges of her massive elbow and strange little whoops that sounded like muted hunting calls.

At last he put down his glass and said mildly, "I trust Miss Burningham was not affected by the heat. What is the matter with her?"

"Nothing that I know of," said the duke in surprise. "She always joins us for meals. What is up with Tilly?"

His wife looked as if she would like to strangle him. Aileen's beautiful face took on a sulky look. The duchess leapt into the awkward silence that had followed her husband's question. "Yes, it was the heat. She's not very strong, you know."

"Dear me," said the marquess. "I would have said she was as strong as an ox."

Aileen giggled. "Oh, I must remember that. Poor old ox, Tilly."

"I trust," said the marquess in even tones, "that you would not repeat anything so cruel. I did not say 'looked like,' I said 'as strong as.'"

Aileen bit her lip and her mother rose majestically from the table. "Shall we leave the gentlemen to their wine, my precious? Don't be too long," she added, waving a roguish finger at her husband. "Fairy's going to play the piano for us."

The marquess groaned inwardly. Would the evening never end? He and the duke sat in silence after the ladies had gone. The duke was working himself up to snatching his guest away from the table as soon as was decently possible, and the marquess was plotting how soon he could make his escape and wishing he were a woman so that he could plead a headache.

All too soon the duke gave a diffident cough and suggested they should join the ladies.

Aileen was already seated at an upright piano. As soon as the marquess was seated she began to sing a selection from *Die Fledermaus* in a high, thin voice, which acted on his nerves like a knife being scraped across the bottom of a pot.

Finally he leapt in with his excuses when she paused for breath. He would need to get an early night. He had a lot to do in the morning.

Plainly disappointed, they reluctantly let him go. He felt guilty and pressed Aileen's hand rather more warmly than he had intended as he made his good-byes. Aileen was immediately transported from a sulky child to a dazzling young woman. She was confident he was in love with her after all and put his long silences of the evening down to manly reticence. She would plot and plan and contrive to get him on his own.

The marquess stood for a moment on the steps outside and took in deep breaths of the now cool evening air. He climbed into his carriage with a sigh of relief and settled back against the leather upholstery, glancing up at the windows of the house as he did so.

He saw Tilly Burningham staring down at him from an upper window, her face lit clearly by the light of an oil lamp. It was flushed and swollen with crying. She raised her hand in a half salute. And then she was gone.

Poor child! he thought as the carriage moved forward. *They deliberately kept her abovestairs.*

He was suddenly weary of the heat of London and of the idle gossip of the Season. He would travel to Paris in the morning and get away from it all for a bit.

CHAPTER FOUR

A week had elapsed since the dinner at the Glenstraith mansion, and the marquess was sitting up in bed in his apartment in the Avenue Foch in Paris, reading the illustrated papers and well content with life.

By his side, still asleep, lay Cora Duval, one of the most beautiful courtesans in Paris. It had been, reflected the marquess, the most satisfactory liaison he had ever entered into, if not the most expensive. Cora was splendid in bed and witty and amusing out of it. He looked down at a copy of the *Illustrated London News* and frowned. There was a picture of Aileen and her friends, taken at Ranelagh, with the usual caption reading, "Enjoying the London Season are . . ." followed by a long list of names. To anyone who did not know the situation it would seem as if Aileen and her friends were enjoying an innocent joke.

The marquess searched on his bedside table, found a magnifying glass, and held it over the picture. The malice in Aileen's eyes seemed to leap out of the page.

Her friends' heads were half turned, and in the strong lens the marquess could make out the object of their mirth. Tilly Burningham was sitting a little behind them with the duchess. She was unbecomingly dressed in a dark gown with a severe collar, and the duchess was leaning toward her with an angry expression on her face. He looked up from the picture as his gentleman's gentleman, Lennox, appeared with the morning post.

He flicked through it until he found himself staring down at a letter from his lawyer. He sliced open the embossed envelope and read the contents.

His lawyer begged to remind his lordship that the month was nearly up, and that if his lordship did not wed soon, he would forfeit his father's fortune.

The marquess swore under his breath. Cora had made him forget the whole cursed business. He picked up the *Illustrated London News* again and stared thoughtfully down at the Ranelagh picture.

I'll marry her, he thought suddenly, *and then I can return to Cora. Tilly won't mind.*

I'll get the fortune, she'll get a home of her own, and then we can go our separate ways.

He leaned over the white length of his mistress's body, revealed by the tossed back bedclothes, and shook one white shoulder gently. "Wake up, my heart," he whispered. "I have to travel to London for a few days. But I shall be back as soon as I have attended to . . . er . . . some unfinished business."

"Do not eat so much, Tilly dear," said Francine. "You'll ruin the figure."

The former Honorable Miss Matilda Burningham would never have dreamed of allowing a servant to address her so familiarly or for that matter stop her from eating a delicious slab of Congress cake. But the present Tilly was deeply grateful for the maid's friendship and, besides, Francine never called her anything other than Miss Burningham in public. She put down her cake with a sigh. "I'm getting as fat as a pig," she groaned.

"You could lose it, oh so easily," said Francine, "if only—"

She broke off as James, the second footman, appeared with an air of suppressed glee and announced in his stateliest voice, "His lordship, the Most Noble Marquess of Heppleford, is in the drawing room and requests a few words with the Honorable Miss Burningham."

Tilly jumped to her feet, nearly oversetting the tea table. "You must be mistaken, James," she gasped. "Surely he wishes to see Lady Aileen!"

"No, miss," said James, dropping his stately manner and grinning all over his face. "It's you he wants, and it couldn't happen at a better time. There's no one else in the house."

Tilly ran to the door.

"Wait!" screamed Francine. "I must do the hair and make the face and change the robe."

"Can't wait!" said Tilly, grinning. "He might get away!"

Francine threw up her hands in despair as Tilly, wearing a skirt and blouse that were coming apart at the waist and with her hair coming down and jam and cake crumbs on her face, hurtled down the stairs to the drawing room.

She hesitated outside the door, wishing she had not been so precipitate, but the butler was already moving to open the double doors of the drawing room, so there was no time to change her mind.

She blinked her eyes before the vision that

was the marquess. A stray sunbeam gilded his golden hair. His suit seemed to have been molded to his body and his embroidered waistcoat emphasized his trim, muscular waist.

"Pray be seated, Miss Burningham," he began. Tilly sat down awkwardly and tried not to slouch. The marquess sat down opposite her with graceful ease, not even looking around to see if the chair was there—a social art Tilly had as yet been unable to accomplish, since she either fell on the floor or hurt her bottom on the edge of the chair.

"It's awfully decent of you to call," said Tilly. "Don't get much callers." She tried to give a coquettish laugh but it emerged as an embarrassed guffaw.

The marquess eyed her coolly. He did not feel in the least embarrassed. He was about to enter into a business contract, that was all.

"Miss Burningham," he said, "you have perhaps heard that under the terms of my late father's will I must marry before the end of the month. That is only a week away and here I am, still unwed."

Tilly's heart began to hammer uncomfortably against her stays.

"So," he went on, "I wondered if you

would do me the honor of becoming my wife?"

Tilly put a hand to her heart, a pathetic feminine gesture in one so robust, and her face drained of color.

"You see," went on the marquess, "I am sure your position in this household is an unhappy one. I am offering you my name and a home of your own—a home rather like Jee-bles—and in return I expect a partner who will fulfill the duties of her position and not . . . er . . . interfere in my affairs."

Tilly opened and shut her mouth. "I wouldn't," she finally gasped. "I mean . . . interfere."

"You do realize it's a sort of business contract?"

"Oh, *yes!*" breathed Tilly, who really didn't understand any such thing.

He stood up, and Tilly stood as well. He moved forward to kiss her on the cheek and then reeled slightly as Tilly gave him a resounding slap on the back.

"It's most awfully ripping of you," she said shyly. "Things are really ghastly here."

"I am afraid we shall have to marry in haste," he said, ignoring the cynical voice in his brain that murmured, *"and repent at leisure."*

Tilly's face fell. "I can't p-pay for the wedding," she stammered, "and I don't like to ask Her Grace."

"There is no need for that," he smiled. "Send all the bills to my lawyer. Ah, I hear the duchess arriving. I had best break the news to her."

At first neither the duchess nor Aileen could quite take in the news, but when it finally got through to them, their astonishment and dismay were ludicrous.

"Well, I ain't paying for the wedding," grumped the duchess sourly. "And I've got too much on my hands to bother with guest lists and all that."

"And I certainly don't want to be maid of honor," said Aileen nastily.

"Nobody asked you," retorted Tilly with a rare burst of spirit.

"Go and get your hat, Tilly," said the marquess quietly. "You are coming with me."

Tilly needed no second bidding and flew from the room.

When she had gone, the marquess turned his icy gaze on the furious duchess. "I am taking Tilly to an old friend of mine," he said. "She will be married from there. I shall send for her trunks later in the day."

"Scheming, conniving thing," said the

duchess, referring to Tilly. "Glad to see the back of her. Never any use anyway. Oh, don't cry, precious."

Aileen was sobbing angrily into a pocket handkerchief.

The marquess swung around with relief as Tilly appeared in the doorway, with a straw boater crammed on her carroty hair.

"Tart!" howled the duchess. "Serpent!"

"Serpent yourself!" said Tilly. "You great hairy cow. You can take that backboard of yours and plonk your great bum on it and sail off down the Thames to oblivion, for all I care."

The marquess winced at the vulgarity and Aileen went into strong hysterics.

"I've a good mind to slap you for your impertinence," said the duchess, lumbering forward threateningly.

"Just you try," gasped Tilly, putting up her small fists, more like a schoolboy than ever. "Come on, then. Let's have you!"

The marquess picked up his enraged fiancée and carried her out of the house and bundled her into his carriage. "That'll larn her," said Tilly, flushed with success.

"By marrying me, you have revenge enough," said the marquess severely. "Now, straighten your hat, sit up straight, and be silent!"

"Yes," said Tilly meekly. "Where are we going?"

"You are going to stay with an old friend of my mother's, a Mrs. Plumb. I thought there might be some trouble, so I called on her before I saw you. She is very old but I could not take you anywhere else, since my relatives would certainly not welcome you. They wished me to keep the marriage—and the money—in the family."

"Were you so sure I would accept?" asked Tilly, suddenly shy.

"Well, yes," he said slowly. "After all, your position was not a happy one. But nonetheless, Tilly, you must curb these exhibitions of unladylike behavior, no matter how severe the provocation. And your language!"

"Spent too much time on the hunting field," said Tilly with an unrepentant grin.

Her spirits were bubbling and soaring like champagne. It was just like a novel. They would be married. She, Tilly Burningham, the Beast, was to marry the Beauty. Love must follow. Why, all her novels told her so!

Mrs. Plumb lived in a great mock Swiss chalet in Fitzjohn's Avenue, just north of Swiss Cottage.

The marquess rang the bell for what seemed an age before the door was opened by an elderly butler.

The butler inclined his head in a stately manner and indicated that they should follow him. He led them through a dark hall to the back of the house and into the garden, where an old lady was snoozing under the shade of a large oak.

"The Honorable Miss Buggering and the Most Nutty Mucker of Heppleford!" announced the butler.

"Don't worry," said the marquess soothingly as he noticed the startled expression on Tilly's face. "He's dotty. Been like that for years. Old lady can't fire him; wouldn't dream of it."

Mrs. Plumb woke up with a start. She was a very frail old lady, dressed in gray lace, lying on a chaise longue like some insubstantial ghost in the bright sunshine.

"Welcome, Philip," she said, offering a withered cheek to be kissed. "And this is . . . ?"

The marquess introduced Tilly, who seized Mrs. Plumb's gloved hand and operated it like a pump handle. "So you are to be Philip's bride," said the old lady, shrinking slightly back into the cushions of the chaise longue, as if to retreat from the boisterous Tilly.

"I'll leave you two ladies to chat," said the marquess unfeelingly, not noticing the dismay on the two faces turned toward him. "I'll see you tomorrow, Tilly. It will be a very quiet wedding, I'm afraid."

"Oh, that's all right," said Tilly hurriedly.

"Yes, please," said Mrs. Plumb faintly. "You may have the conservatory for the reception. So little there to damage."

She held out her hand to be kissed by the marquess and then lay back against the cushions and closed her eyes.

Left alone, Tilly eyed her nervously. "Jolly ripping of you to have me," she ventured.

"You must excuse me. I must sleep," said Mrs. Plumb, opening her faded blue eyes. "Tell Jumbles—the butler, you know—to show you to your rooms. You must be exhausted."

Tilly reluctantly complied, although she would have liked to stay in the fresh air of the garden with its bright flowers and cool grass.

The butler was nowhere to be seen and she suddenly did not have the courage to poke around strange servants' quarters looking for him. She finally came across a startled betweenstairs maid who conducted her to a pleasant suite of rooms on the second floor. The furniture belonged to the eighties of the last century, being of the hot, overstuffed variety. But a great elm tree grew right outside the windows of both sitting room and bedroom, shielding them from the brassy glare outside.

Tilly kicked off her shoes and lay down on the bed, clasping her hands behind her neck and staring up at the ceiling.

Bit by bit her excitement began to fade, to be replaced by cold doubt. Already she missed Francine's reassuring presence. And what would she, Tilly, wear as a wedding gown? There would surely be no time to get one made and even Tilly knew one simply did not wear ready-made clothes, particularly to one's wedding.

Then she remembered she had her mother's wedding dress in an old trunk with the rest of her belongings, which were being sent for. It would just have to do.

The marquess returned briefly that evening to tell her the wedding was set for a week ahead. He was pleasant, smiling, and businesslike. Mrs. Plumb appeared to have detached herself from the whole proceedings and Tilly was left to handle much of the arrangements for the wedding herself.

She was sorely in need of another woman to talk to, to advise her, to allay her fears. The marquess's formidable aunts and their disappointed daughters were to attend, but they were of no help.

One evening during the following week, Tilly carried her mother's wedding dress downstairs to ask Mrs. Plumb for her advice. But Mrs. Plumb had merely glanced at it through half-closed eyes and murmured, "Very pretty."

Tilly longed for the courage to consult a dressmaker, but the bills were already heading in the marquess's direction for food and flowers and wine and extra servants, since the servants in Mrs. Plumb's mansion were mostly too old to cope with the added work and fuss.

Then there was the cost of the marquee to be erected in the garden and the fashionable orchestra to be paid.

The weather blazed on remorselessly and the letters to *The Times* prophecied drought.

It was a very hot and tired Tilly who finally stood at the altar for the wedding rehearsal. The marquess arrived with Toby, who was to perform the part of best man. Both seemed in high spirits—in more ways than one, to judge from the strong smell of brandy emanating from them.

Tilly's maid of honor was a timid, quiet girl, an acquaintance from Tilly's Jeebles days, called Bessie Cartwright-Smythe. Tilly went through her part of the ceremony, anxious that she should not do anything wrong.

The marquess and Toby left immediately afterward to attend a bachelor party in the marquess's honor, the silent Bessie went off to stay with an aunt, and Tilly was once more on her own. An old friend of her father's, Colonel Percy Braithwaite, was to give her away and was spending the evening at his club.

The eve of her wedding!

She lay on the chaise longue in the garden, staring up at the faintly moving leaves of the oak tree, feeling increasingly nervous. She had not yet even tried on her mother's wedding dress.

She thought of her husband-to-be with a sort of half-formed adolescent longing. If only he would smile at her tenderly—even hold her hand. He surely could not be indifferent to her, thought poor Tilly, unaware that that was the very reason that had prompted the marquess to propose.

I shall probably sleep with him, thought

Tilly, feeling very warm at the thought. *But what on earth am I supposed to do? The duchess always says that only the lower classes feel passion—witness the Fallen Women—but all my romances are about lords and ladies. Perhaps he is distant with me because he feels it would be ill-bred to betray his feelings. And babies! He will want an heir. But how is it achieved? Surely not like the farm animals. Oh, these are dreadful thoughts. . . .*

And so Tilly's mind raced on and on as a cool sliver of moon rose above the baking city.

After awhile she felt her eyelids begin to droop and she reluctantly took herself off to her hot bedroom. As she was dropping off to sleep an anguished thought struck her. She had forgotten to hire the services of a major-domo to announce the guests and she shuddered to think of the muddle old Jumbles would make with their names. And then she fell into a deep nightmare in which the marquess, aided by Aileen and the duchess, was pushing her into a home for Disreputable Women because she had betrayed too strong a passion for her husband.

The day of Tilly's wedding dawned brassy and hotter than ever. She was awakened at dawn by the energetic hammering of the men erecting the marquee in the garden.

She dressed and went downstairs to find the house abustle with strange servants carrying chairs, potted plants, and silver. Mrs. Plumb appeared early as well, roused at last to a sense of her duties to her young guest. Tilly was bustled back upstairs with Mrs. Plumb's antique lady's maid to begin the long and painful preparations for the wedding ceremony.

It was all too soon discovered that Tilly's wedding dress had been designed to fit her mother's slim figure. A servant was sent scuttling off to find a seamstress, and Tilly stood miserably while the dress was sewn onto her around two-inch inserts of white satin. The gown had also been designed to cover an 1880s bustle, and there was an agonizing search of the attics before the right undergarment was found.

Despite Tilly's protests, white enamel makeup, complete with two circles of rouge, one on either cheek, was considered de rigueur for a bride.

Tilly was poked and pushed and turned and pinned and painted and frizzed and finally drowned in Parma Violets, a perfume that always made her sneeze.

The seamstress, the lady's maid, and a bevy of other female servants who had been dragged in to help finally ceased their efforts and stood in a circle, staring at Tilly in satisfaction.

They had turned Tilly into a fashion plate —but a fashion plate of the 1880s, not the present early 1900s. Not a hair was out of place. The creamy folds of old lace were swept into a large bustle at the back. A little coronet of artificial white flowers held a short veil of fine and priceless Valenciennes lace. A huge bouquet in a silver filigree holder was put into her white-gloved hands and she was propelled toward the door. Between the old-fashioned dress and the enameled mask of her makeup, Tilly looked like a pretty but lifeless waxwork from Madame Tussauds.

But to Mrs. Plumb and the colonel and all the servants lined up at the foot of the stairs, Tilly looked perfect. Compliments were showered on her, all of which Tilly accepted with gruff gratitude.

But as Tilly walked up the aisle, the marquess's relatives let out gasps of delighted shock and dismay. What a fright the awful girl looked! How clumsily she walked with those great mannish strides! The marquess gave his bride a warm smile. He had wanted to shock his relatives and dear Tilly was doing just that, *splendidly*.

All Tilly's doubts and fears were swept away the minute the marquess bent to kiss her. His lips were cool and firm, her own, warm and naively passionate.

She walked down the aisle on his arm, oblivious of the hard stares, deaf to the spiteful comments. The "Wedding March" boomed triumphantly from the organ loft and the bells in the Norman tower crashed and clanged their joyous message to the world.

The Honorable Matilda Burningham had made it.

She had captured the best-looking man in London.

She was a marchioness.

"I feel like Cinderella," said the Marchioness of Heppleford shyly.

No response from her husband.

Tilly sighed and looked out of the window of the carriage to where the great pile of Chennington lay with its medieval spires and battlements standing up against a purple-black sky. The sun was dying behind the thunder-laden clouds in fiery splendor, gilding the gray stone of Chennington with a strange light.

In the calm before the storm, the park through which they were driving seemed extra green, the heavy old trees standing motionless in the sultry heat.

A white swan bent its long neck to study its reflection in an ornamental lake beside the drive, and the weeping willows seemed to twine branches with their mirror counterparts in the flat black water. A marble rotunda gleamed white on its grassy hillock.

The marquess shifted uneasily in the carriage. What a farce of a wedding! That terrible butler, Jumbles, murdering the names of the guests with gay abandon (and the marquess was sure it was neither age nor eccentricity on the part of the butler but hell-inspired mischief that had prompted him to announce the acid Duchess of Dereham as "the Dutchman of Drearie"), and Tilly, chattering and romping like a schoolgirl.

He had promised the delicious Cora that he would be back in her arms by tomorrow at the latest. He would catch the Channel steamer from Southampton this evening, he decided. It *was* his wedding night, but then, this was not a normal wedding and Tilly was such a strange girl, she would probably find nothing amiss.

The staff of Chennington was lined up in the great hall under the moldering banners of dead and gone Hepplefords to greet the young bride.

Tilly had been used to a large staff of servants at Jeebles, so the formidable array of faces did not daunt her. The marquess noticed that she said the correct thing to each member of his staff and that nagging feeling of guilt about leaving her so soon returned to plague him.

But when Tilly arrived in the long drawing room with its gilded walls and painted ceiling, wearing a suit of a mannish cut, in a shocking shade of pink that argued violently with her hair, he fortified himself from the decanter and became more determined than ever to make his escape.

Tilly chattered happily about a visit from the housekeeper, Mrs. Judd, who had promised to take her on a tour of the mansion on the morrow.

The marquess put down his glass with a little click.

"Tilly, my dear," he said, "I must leave for Paris this very evening."

All animation disappeared from Tilly's

face. The thunder rumbled outside and a vivid flash of lightning flared in the darkening room.

"Business?" asked Tilly, her own voice sounding harsh and strange in her ears.

"Yes, business."

"Then . . . I cannot keep you."

"No."

They sat in silence, Tilly's heartbroken, the Marquess's embarrassed, while outside the full fury of the storm burst over the mansion.

"You can't travel in this weather," said Tilly at last.

"I must."

Tilly could feel the weak and treacherous tears forming at the back of her eyes. She was to be a wife in name only, after all. The other half of the business contract.

She rose stiffly, as if her whole body were in pain. The exuberant schoolgirl enthusiasm had gone from her voice. "Then I beg you to excuse me," she said. "I must lie down."

The marquess crossed the long room and held the door open for her. She walked past him to the staircase, where she paused with her hand on the carved bannister and looked back.

Again the marquess had the odd feeling that Tilly was two women. A beautiful ghost seemed to move wraithlike in the dim and shadowy hall in front of Tilly's face, in front of Tilly's wide, pain-filled eyes.

Then she turned and walked slowly up the staircase, her head held high.

"We have a bargain, haven't we?" The marquess suddenly called out. "Haven't we?"

But only the sound of tumbling and crashing thunder came in reply.

CHAPTER FIVE

On the following day, when the fireworks of the storm had given way to damp drizzle, the county called at Chennington in droves to pay their respects to the new bride, only to be told that "my lady was indisposed." Where, then, was my lord? "Indisposed also," said his lordship's venerable butler, Masters. The servants had taken an immediate liking to Tilly and felt their beloved master was behaving shamefully.

So the county turned their carriages around and trotted off down the drive under the great dripping trees. But they talked and they speculated.

On the third day after the marquess's departure the blow fell in the servants' hall. Mr. Masters read the social columns in one of the lower orders of newspapers. In a hushed voice, he read the offending paragraph out to the cook, Mrs. Comfrey. Over a glass of blackberry brandy, the cook subsequently read the news to the housekeeper, Mrs. Judd, and the three gathered in the housekeeper's cosy parlor that evening for a council of war.

"It doesn't make sense," said Mr. Masters. "I've known his lordship since he was a boy and I'd never have dreamed he would do anything like this. His lordship has always been the soul of kindness and consideration."

"That trollop! And a foreigner too!" cried Mrs. Judd, clutching the newspaper to her black bombazine bosom.

"Here, let's have a proper look at it, then," said the cook, reaching out a chubby red hand and taking the newspaper. "You only read it to me."

Her steel-rimmed spectacles perched on the end of her stubby nose, the cook traced the print with her finger and read aloud:

"Strange Wedding Night for Peer of the Realm.

It is rumored that the handsome Marquess of Heppleford left the arms of his bride two hours after the wedding to fly to the experienced arms of one of Paris's most notorious ladies of easy virtue, a certain Mademoiselle Cora Duval, until lately under the protection of the Compt du Chervenix. Visitors to the marquess's stately home have been turned away with the intelligence that the new marchioness is indisposed. No wonder! We shudder to think of the affect of such behavior on the lower orders. A solid, virtuous family life is the backbone of our nation. It is up to our Ruling Class to set a good example. . .

"Well, I never!" said the cook. "And there's my poor lady shut up in her room and hardly touching any of the food I've sent up to her."

"What on earth can she *do?*" moaned Mrs. Judd. "How can a decent girl like that compete with a—a—*Scarlet Woman?*"

"For the moment, she needs to keep herself occupied," said Mr. Masters, smoothing back the silver wings of his hair. "Young ladies in her situation who don't keep themselves busy—know what happens to them?"

"No! What?" chorused his audience.

"They goes into a decline, that's what!"

"Oh, mercy!"

"So here's what I suggest we do. Mrs. Judd will go up to my lady's room in the morning and will tell her that the old marquess's rooms in the East Wing need to be cleaned out. They do, as a matter of fact. Mrs. Judd will ask her whether she would like to look at the furniture and ornaments and stuff to see if there's anything she would like for the downstairs' rooms. My lady was brought up proper, so she'll have a sense of duty, so mind you tell her it's expected of her, Mrs. Judd.

"And burn all the newspapers."

"But if we get her roused and about and someone comes calling, maybe she'll learn that way," protested the cook.

Mr. Masters raised his bushy eyebrows in surprise. "Mrs. Comfrey, you forget we are dealing with the aristocracy here. None of them would dream of saying anything so spiteful!"

Masters had guessed Tilly's sense of duty correctly. She emerged from her seclusion, pale and heavy-eyed. The old marquess's rooms were chockablock with papers and bric-a-brac, and Tilly picked up things list-lessly and put them down again in a helpless kind of way until the housekeeper's en-thusiasm began to infect her. Mrs. Judd ex-claimed in delight over the discovery of a beautiful Ming vase that was lying under a rolltop desk. The late marquess had used the vase as an exotic deposit for everything from rubber bands to paper clips and unanswered correspondence.

After that find, it turned into a sort of treasure hunt and Tilly became quite flushed and animated to find a clutch of valuable Dresden figurines in the coal scuttle. Like most housekeepers of stately homes, Mrs. Judd had a knowledge of art and china that would have rivaled that of a museum curator.

"At least someone seems to have tidied up the papers on the desk," remarked Tilly.

"That would be the lawyer," said Mrs. Judd. "Ever such a search there was for the will. We knew there *was* a will, of course, because me and Mr. Masters were witnesses. Not that we knew what was in it, for it wouldn't have been fitting, like, for us to read it. Imagine it turning up in the library! But right glad I was that it did. For you'll never believe it, but that bold Rosy Jenkins down at the Crown—that's the landlord of the public house's girl, down in the village—well, she was going about telling folks as how the old marquess came down one night and asked her and her dad to witness his will. 'Bite your tongue, my girl,' I says to her, I says. As if his lordship ever visited a public house!

"But Rosy always was a little liar, if you'll forgive me for speaking so open, my lady. Why, I remember the time when MacTavish —that's the gardener—caught her thieving apples from the orchard in broad daylight, and she turns round on him as bold as brass and says they're her own apples what she brought along for a picnic.

"Now, this here, my lady, is the late lordship's—God rest his soul—dressing case what he took with him when he traveled. All gold fittings. Perhaps my lord would like to have it—What's this? Well, I *never!*"

Mrs. Judd had opened the dressing case and was staring at a folded piece of parchment. On it, in bold gothic letters, was the legend LAST WILL AND TESTAMENT.

Mrs. Judd crackled open the parchment and stared at the signatures, then at the date, and she suddenly sat down on the floor with her hand pressed to her corseted bosom.

"It do be queer, my lady," she said as Tilly stared in amazement, "but that there Rosy was telling the truth. This is a later will than the one that was found in the library. Don't you think you'd better read it, my lady?"

"No!" said Tilly in a harsh voice. "Considering the contents of the other will, I shudder to think what the old geezer put in this one. Probably," she added bitterly, "my husband does not inherit unless he cuts my head off two months after the marriage."

"Oh, don't take on so, my lady," said Mrs. Judd. "His old lordship was all right in his head, although he did have his peculiar little ways."

"Do you know my husband's address in Paris?" asked Tilly abruptly.

"Yes, my lady."

"Then send . . . that . . . example of the noble marquess's peculiar little ways to him. It's his affair, not mine."

"My lady," came Masters's voice from the doorway. "Her Grace, the Duchess of Glenstraith, and Lady Aileen Dunbar have called. Shall I tell them you are indisposed?"

"No," said Tilly, thinking quickly. She might be husbandless but at least she was mistress of this splendid home and no longer a penniless companion to be bullied. "I shall receive them. Where have you put them?"

"In the drawing room, my lady."

"Lead the way," said Tilly, straightening her shoulders.

It was only after she had entered the drawing room that Tilly realized she should have

109

changed. Her hair was coming down and there was a smut on the end of her nose.

The duchess was dressed in a tailored suit of a particularly noisy tartan. Her heavy face was free of its usual bristling hairs. Next to her on a Chesterfield sat Aileen, looking very jaunty in a sailor suit and a white straw hat embellished with red china cherries.

"Well, you haven't changed, Tilly," barked the duchess. "Still a mess."

Tilly remained standing. "And how are you, Your Grace?" she asked sweetly. "Shaved, I see."

"There's no need to be offensive," snapped the duchess, turning purple.

"Oh, really?" said Tilly, raising her brows. "You just were, you know."

"This was a mistake," said the Duchess of Glenstraith. "You always were an ill-bred girl and your present unhappiness does not excuse your rudeness."

"Poor Tilly," sighed Aileen. "I am engaged to Toby Bassett, you know. But perhaps in your present misery you do not wish to hear of anyone else's good fortune."

"What misery?" snapped Tilly. "What rot is this?"

"If you don't know, Tilly dear, then I certainly shall be the last to tell you. There's no need for you to be so cross. We were in the neighborhood and only dropped by to hold your hand."

Tilly marched to the window and stared out. A muddy traveling carriage was drawn up outside the house. "You didn't drop in, you vultures," she said, swinging around. "You traveled especially from London to relay some piece of spiteful codswallop. So out with it!"

"I wouldn't *dream* of it," said Aileen with her maddening silvery laugh. "Come, Mama! We are obviously not welcome."

"Wait a bit!" said Tilly, standing squarely in front of them. "What about my wages?"

"Your wages!" gasped the duchess. "And you with all this. Oh, selfish child!"

Tilly pushed her chin forward until her face was almost touching that of the duchess. "You owe me wages," she said coldly. "You will send them to me or I shall sue. It'll look great in the newspapers . . . the great and charitable Duchess of Glenstraith won't pay a working girl!"

"Come, Mama," said Aileen again. "You must excuse Tilly. She is smarting at seeing her own name in the newspapers."

Aileen and her mother moved toward the doors, which were quickly swung open by

Masters before they could reach them. The cook could be seen sliding quickly through the green baize door at the far side of the hall, and the black skirt of the housekeeper flickered nimbly along the upper landing.

The duchess paused in the hallway. "I just want to say one thing to you, Tilly. I—"

"Oh, make a noise like a hoop and bowl off," snapped Tilly, turning on her heel and retreating to the drawing room. She slammed the doors behind her and stood with her back against them, feeling her heart thudding against her ribs. Then she saw the folded newspaper lying coyly on the sofa, where it had been left by her visitors.

It seemed to take her a very long time to walk across the room and pick up the newspaper. STRANGE WEDDING NIGHT FOR PEER OF THE REALM seemed to leap at her from the page.

She read it slowly and carefully and then read it again. Then she sat down and clutched her stomach. *I can't bear any more of this pain,* thought Tilly. *I won't!*

The portraits of the Hepplefords stared down at her in disdain. Tilly raised her head and stared back. "No, damn you," she cried, shaking her fist at their painted faces. "I'll get even with you Hepplefords yet." She rose and rang the bell.

Masters appeared as imperturbable as ever.

"My lady?"

"I have a traveling carriage, I assume?" said Tilly, striding up and down the room. "A fast one?"

"There is his lordship's Renault . . . his new motorcar, my lady. Gaskell, the chauffeur, handles her very well, but it is an open car, my lady, and the weather is inclement."

"Blow the weather," said Tilly. "I won't melt. Get the car round."

Tilly paced up and down the drive some fifteen minutes later, swathed in an ulster and with a yellow sou'wester on her head, fretting with impatience while Gaskell lit the acetylene lamps, for the day was dark.

Finally the engine was turning over and Tilly climbed in the back.

"London, Gaskell!" cried the Marchioness of Heppleford, hanging on to her hat. "And don't spare the horsepower!"

Some thirty minutes later, the Duchess of Glenstraith's carriage horses neighed and bridled as two speed-mad fiends hurtled past the carriage at thirty miles per hour.

"Maniacs!" yelled the duchess, thrusting

her great head and shoulders through the carriage window.

She did not know that Tilly was hell-bent on reaching the Glenstraith town house before the duchess arrived home.

Some four hours later Gaskell was moodily polishing the lamps of the car outside the Duchess of Glenstraith's house and wondering whether his mistress was mad. He was soaked to the skin, but had refused to go indoors to dry himself at the kitchen fire. He loved the Renault more than anything in his life and shuddered to think what might happen to it if he left it alone for a minute. The rain had stopped, but black and heavy clouds piling up behind the buildings promised a deluge to come. "It's all right for her ladyship," grumbled Gaskell to himself. She was partly protected by the hood at the back, but he had to brave the elements unprotected in the front. *Funny,* he mused, *I wouldn't have thought her ladyship would be thoughtless where servants were concerned.* He broke off his musings as the door of the mansion opened and Tilly appeared, followed by a young female who was carrying a battered suitcase.

"Home!" said Tilly triumphantly.

As if in answer the heavens opened and Gaskell steered the car through the glistening streets, feeling as if he were piloting a ship on a stormy sea.

But he got a surprise one mile outside the limits of the city. Tilly called to him to stop at a large and comfortable-looking inn. Then she issued brisk instructions. Gaskell was to pay the ostler to look after his beloved car by putting it somewhere under cover. Then he, Gaskell, was to go directly upstairs to the bedchamber that Tilly would reserve for him, divest himself of his wet clothes, and give them to the chambermaid to dry and she, Tilly, would send him up a substantial meal.

Having seen to these arrangements and having brushed aside the startled and voluble thanks of the delighted Gaskell, Tilly settled down in the inn parlor and looked with satisfaction at her companion.

"Won't that old trout be as mad as fire when she finds you've scarpered," she said.

Francine stared at her severely. "You must not use such schoolboyish expressions, Tilly."

"Oh, don't change me *now,*" wailed Tilly. "Wait until we get home. But, tell me again, Francine. Do you think you can do it?"

Francine looked at the flushed and earnest

face opposite her. "Of course," she said calmly. "I, Francine, am the best lady's maid ever. It will be . . . how you call it . . . ? a challenge. But you must do everything I say, my lady."

"I'd rather you call me Tilly, like you used to," said Tilly shyly. "I've been pretty lonely."

"No," said Francine, "it would not be *comme il faut*. What if one of your servants should hear me?"

"Oh, all right," said Tilly, crinkling up her eyes.

"*That* will have to go for a start, my lady," said Francine. "That trick with the eyes. You have very pretty eyes, but how can anyone see them when you twist them so?"

"You'll do," said Tilly happily. "I'll change, you'll see. Philip won't recognize me when he comes home . . . if he ever comes home."

Rebellion had arisen in Tilly's much humiliated breast after she had read the newspaper item. The blood of her battling ancestors had seemed to course in her veins. She was not going to go down without fighting. It had struck her that perhaps Francine's undoubted genius could transform her in some way. The startled Francine had

116

agreed. There was, she had said, enough raw material to work on. And the clever Francine knew that by the time she was finished with Tilly, then she, Francine, would be famous among ladies' maids.

She suddenly looked sympathetically across at Tilly, who was eating huge slices of fruitcake as if they were going to be her last (*Which they are,* thought Francine), and said, "I can promise you beauty, my lady. I cannot promise you love."

"Just give me the one," said Tilly, "and I'll just see what I can do about the other."

The Marquess of Heppleford was suffering from burnt-out passion and a guilty conscience. He sat at his desk in the apartment in the Avenue Foch and stared moodily at the pile of unopened correspondence on his desk. He had just spent what should have been two glorious weeks with his mistress in the South of France, but the whole thing had been haunted by Tilly's hurt face and accusing eyes.

As his man unpacked his trunks he opened the first letter with a sigh. It was from one of his aunts, Lady Mary Swingleton. Pinned to the top of the letter was that cutting from the newspaper. Underneath, Lady Mary had given vent to her lacerated feelings: That the marquess should marry this freak of a girl was bad enough, but that he should have the family name dragged through the columns of the gutter press was outside of enough!

The marquess crumpled it and threw it into the wastepaper basket. He picked up the next one and opened it.

Much to his surprise, his father's will fell out, accompanied by a brief note from his steward explaining how the will had been found. The marquess read it slowly. "'A most ingenious paradox,'" he quoted bitterly. Then he picked up the will again. "Let me see," he muttered. "Who gets the moneybags if I don't comply with the terms? Cyril Nettleford! My god, over my dead body." Cyril Nettleford, his nephew, was a spotty youth with doubtful sexual tastes and worse manners.

I shall contest it, thought the marquess, *though I don't think it'll do much good. I'm supposed to show evidence of an heir within twelve months! What will my beloved wife say to that? Probably, "Oh, rats!"*

He leaned back in his chair and called to his man, "Pack the bags again. We're leaving for home."

Home.

He had a sudden vision of Chennington with its quiet rooms and cool lawns. Then the picture was marred by a vision of Tilly. His home was no longer his own. He now had to share it with a tomboy who would no doubt rebuke him for his well-broadcast infidelity in the language of the stables.

His gentleman's gentleman, Lennox, coughed discreetly. "Does your lordship wish to apprise her ladyship of our return?"

"No. Oh, damn it, *yes.*"

Had Tilly seen the newspaper? he wondered. No doubt some well-meaning friend would tell her. Yet, after all, he had nothing to feel guilty about. They had a business arrangement. But he should never have caused her such humiliation. He would make it up to her, he decided.

And then he remembered that he had to produce an heir.

"He's coming home," cried Tilly, dancing into the drawing room and waving a marconi-gram. "He's coming home!" She smiled and crinkled up her eyes, and received a glass of iced water straight in the face.

As she choked and sputtered Francine put down the glass and said grimly, "I had to do it, my lady. Shock tactics. You must never again twist the eyes up so. *Jamais!*"

"Oh, Francine, you are a slave driver," moaned Tilly, dabbing her eyes with the towel that Francine had handed to her. "I'm absolutely starving, my eyes are sore from reading, my back is sore from sitting up so straight, I'm tired of mock dinners and mock tea parties, and I'd like to go riding."

"Not yet," was all Francine would say. "It is time for your rehearsal, and you must pretend it is real." She rang the bell on the wall beside her and a group of ten servants, including Masters, the butler, and Mrs. Judd, the housekeeper, came in.

"Now," said Francine, smoothing down the folds of her new black silk gown, "you must all pretend you are actors and that I am your producer. Lady Tilly, this is your house party and you must work the imagination and pretend these are your guests. Now, begin!"

The servants enjoyed these mock parties immensely and played their parts with gusto. Mrs. Judd made a formidable duchess; Mr. Masters a boring elder statesmen; and James, the second footman, a wild young man whose conversation showed an alarming tendency to become too intimate. Among them they managed to represent all the social embarrassments that Tilly might meet, while Francine carefully listened and schooled Tilly's replies.

Francine looked at her protégée with some complacency—as well she might. Rigorous dieting and the right sort of exercise had melted away Tilly's puppy fat like magic, leaving her with a slim figure, rounded in the right places. Her red hair was brushed until it shone and fell in soft, natural waves on her forehead. Her skin was creamy with only a faint blush of pink on her cheeks, which owed nothing to art. She was wearing a high-collared dress of smoky-blue tulle that emphasized the blue of her eyes. Her gown had the latest thing in hobble skirts, the narrow hemline, as the lady's maid pointed out, being an excellent device for curbing Tilly's long mannish strides.

At last the rehearsal was over and Tilly was flushed with success, for Francine had hardly had to correct her at all.

"Now we will have a *real* house party for his lordship's return," said Francine.

Tilly's face fell in disappointment. "I—I wanted to be alone with him," she said shyly.

"And what good would that do?" asked the lady's maid. "It is better that he sees you in a crowd of people first. The men, they always want what is elusive. And we shall ask the duchess and her so-horrible *fille.*"

"Oh, no!" wailed Tilly. "Anyone but them. Anyway, they won't come."

"Yes, they will," said Francine. "They will want to see exactly how your marriage has failed."

"Mr. Toby Bassett," announced Masters.

Francine whipped up her workbasket, escaped to a chair in the corner of the room, and then bent her black head over her work, looking the very picture of a correct lady's maid.

Tilly rose gracefully to her feet. "Mr. Bassett!" she exclaimed in a soft voice, quite unlike her usual ringing tones. "To what do we owe this pleasure?"

Toby sat down suddenly on the nearest chair, holding his hat and cane, since society decreed that a gentleman should never surrender hat and cane to the butler on making a call, as it might imply that he meant to stay longer than the prescribed time.

He looked at Tilly with his familiar brooding stare.

"You *are* Miss Burningham . . . I mean, you are Philip's wife, aren't you?"

Tilly gave a light, silvery laugh that ran carefully up the scale and down again. Mrs.

Humphry, in her book *Manners for Women,* which Tilly had studied at length, said,

> There is no greater ornament to conversation than the ripple of silvery notes that forms the perfect laugh. It makes the person who evokes it feel pleased with himself, and even invests what he has said with a charm of wit and humor that might not be otherwise observed.

But Toby continued to smolder at her and in no way looked pleased with himself, so Tilly said lightly, "Don't I look the same, Mr. Bassett?"

"No, you don't," said Toby. "In fact, you look like all the other ladies . . . you know, pretty."

Tilly glowed with pleasure and said, "Thank you," although she felt his remark had not been meant as a compliment.

There was an awkward silence. Then Tilly remembered Masters's maxim. *"If conversation fails, my lady, ring for tea."*

Tea gave Tilly a splendid opportunity to watch how the elegant Mr. Bassett was able to roll up and eat tiny cucumber sandwiches without getting any butter on his gloves. She wondered if he were able to do the same drunk, for she realized that perhaps some of the strangeness emanating from Mr. Bassett was because he was stone-cold sober.

"Is Philip home?" asked Toby.

"No," replied Tilly. "But I had a marconigram from him this morning. He is traveling from Paris to London to see his lawyers and then he will be arriving here. I am sending out invitations to a house party to celebrate his arrival. Perhaps you would—"

"Yes, I will. Love to. Great. Splendid. My bags are out in the carriage. I'll tell my man to get 'em," said Toby, roused to rare enthusiasm.

She waited while he left to see to the arrangement of his trunks, and Francine murmured from her corner, "He is escaping from something, that one . . . perhaps from some *one.* Congratulate him on his engagement."

"Commiserate, more likely," said Tilly. But as Toby reappeared, minus hat, gloves, and cane this time, she duly offered her congratulations on his engagement to Lady Aileen.

Toby visibly paled and his face took on a hunted look. "Very kind of you," he said, nonetheless, in his usual impeccable drawl.

Out of the corner of her eye she saw Francine was making drinking motions, and so

Tilly asked him if he would like something stronger.

"I can't," said Toby wildly, looking more like the young Byron than ever. "I promised Aileen. And her mother has enrolled me in the Toward the Light and Away from the Bottle Society. She's on the committee," he added unnecessarily, for Her Grace appeared to be on the committee of everything.

"And does this society help?" asked Tilly.

"I can't understand it," he said, losing his usual lethargic elegance and running his fingers through his curls. "I get served with a cup of tea and one white, hard, iced cake with a brown fern painted on the top in mud-colored icing. Then everyone laughs a lot and is very jolly, and on my first attendance, a large, jolly sort of woman wagged a finger under my nose and asked me if I had found Jesus Christ. I said I hadn't lost him and she said, 'Oh, what a wag you rips are!' which I thought was most ghastly, frightfully rude, you know. And then they show lantern slides all about a man who kicks his children and beats his wife, and when he's not doing that, he's in the boozer, kicking his friends and beating them, and then he sees the light, which is a sort of sunbeam with a great scaly angel in a nightgown hanging around it, you know, and he claps his forehead and falls on his knees and smashes up all the bottles in the boozer. And then you see him out in the world, preaching to the drunken sinners and kicking and beating them when they won't listen, so I ask myself, What's the difference?" Toby paused for breath and looked hopefully at Tilly.

Tilly tried to hide an enormous grin, particularly when she heard a discreet cough from the lady's maid. After all, the redoubtable Mrs. Humphry had been very definite about grins:

> As to grins, very few of them can be, in the remotest sense of the word, described as pleasing. Pretty teeth may redeem some of them from absolute ignomony, but, as a rule, the exhibition of whole meadows of pale pink gums is inconsonant with one's ideas of beauty.

"Well, can't you just stop on your own?" she eventually asked.

Toby shook his head with some pride. "It's the family failing, you see," he explained. "I come from a long line of tipplers."

Francine was making walking movements

with her fingers across the top of her work-basket.

"You must excuse me, Mr. Bassett," said Tilly, rising to her feet and swaying slightly to get her balance on a pair of very high heels. "We shall meet at dinner. Masters will show you to your rooms."

She curtsied gracefully as Toby stood up and swept from the room, followed by her maid.

But there was no rest for Tilly that afternoon and dressing for dinner was to be a scrambled affair. The guests had to be at Chennington as soon as possible, Francine had said. So invitations were quickly written and dispatched by messenger to various members of the local county. Gaskell was sent up to London to deliver an invitation to the duchess and family. Then with the help of Francine, Tilly scrambled into a dinner gown of sleek black panel velvet trimmed with jet. It was an extremely sophisticated dress for such a young girl, but the new Tilly carried it with an air. A pair of long crimson kid gloves and a crimson ostrich-feather fan with diamond-studded sticks completed the ensemble. Tilly twisted and turned in front of the looking glass. "Don't you think I look a bit like a French tart?" she asked doubtfully.

"A very well-bred one, my lady," said Francine, "and infinitely seductive."

For the first time, the startling combination of Tilly's bright-red hair, white skin, and blue eyes was shown to advantage.

"I-I don't want to look seductive for anyone but Philip," said Tilly, hesitating

"Nonsense!" said Francine affectionately. "Of course you do. Your sophisticated husband is a man of the world, *hein?* And he will notice how men look at you now."

"Oh, well," sighed Tilly, picking up her train, "I'd better get on with it."

"No, my lady," said the maid severely, "you do not leave this room with your train bundled over your arm like a pile of washing. Drop your train. Now begin again. No! No! Here, let me show you. Now like that. *So.* Walk backward and forward. Good. Now the fan. No! *No!* You wave it, you do not flap it! Again . . . again. Good! *Now,* you may go."

Toby rose slowly to his feet and gazed at the vision in red and black, framed in the doorway of the drawing room. He felt strangely breathless and excited and began to think that being sober might not be so bad after all.

CHAPTER SIX

The Marquess of Heppleford was an extremely puzzled man. Various strange servants were sorting out mountains of luggage in the hall. Various strange carriages were being led off to the stables.

"What is all this?" he asked Masters as that gentleman welcomed him home.

"The members of the house party arrived this morning, my lord," murmured Masters, relieving his lordship of his hat and cane.

"Indeed!" The marquess's lips folded in a thin line. "Tell my lady I wish to see her immediately."

"I am afraid that is not possible, my lord," said Masters soothingly. "My lady has taken her guests on a picnic."

"Where the hell are they, then? Where have they gone?"

"I am afraid I do not know, my lord. My

lady did not tell me. But you will see her ladyship at dinner."

The marquess crashed up to his rooms in a bad mood. He had been looking forward to peace and quiet, not a houseful of guests. Then there was the question of the will. His lawyer had said it would not be a good idea to contest it and, after all, he had added delicately, my lord was already married and would . . . er . . . naturally wish an heir.

How can I tell Tilly about this new will with all these bloody people around? he thought crossly. He lay down on the bed, planning only to rest for a few minutes, but he was tired from his travels and fell asleep, to be aroused only some three hours later by the sound of the dressing gong from the hall below.

With the assistance of his man, he dressed himself in white tie and tails and marched along the corridor to his wife's rooms and rattled the doorknob.

"Who's there?" called a light, feminine voice he did not recognize.

He stood, frowning, and then called, "Heppleford! Who's that?"

There was a delicious ripple of laughter from behind the door and then that tantalizing voice said, "It's I, Tilly, Philip dear. You must not see me until I am dressed. I will see you downstairs. The guests are in the drawing room."

"I don't know who you are," said Heppleford, "but you can tell my wife that I do not like these silly schoolgirlish jokes."

Silence answered him and he slammed noisily off downstairs. He blinked at the array of guests in his drawing room. It was a beautiful evening and the long windows were opened. There were about fifteen people, including, he noticed with increasing bad temper, the ducal family Glenstraith. He moved from group to group murmuring his greetings and then seized Toby Bassett by the arm and half dragged him onto the terrace.

"What the hell is going on here?" he demanded. "Has Tilly run mad? What are the horrible Glenstraiths doing here?"

"Steady on!" protested Toby. "I'm engaged to Aileen."

The marquess took a step back and stared at his friend, who was gazing mournfully into a glass of lemonade. "She trapped you when you were drunk," said the marquess. "Out with it, Toby."

After some gentlemanly hesitation, Toby began to talk, and, once having started, he couldn't seem to stop. Aileen and her mother

131

had indeed trapped him with champagne and moonlight. Before he knew where he was, he had been *told* by the duchess that he had proposed to Aileen, although he could not remember it. Then he complained at equal length of his enforced temperance, ending up with a cry from the heart. "What am I to do? If it had been some stunning female like Tilly, I could understand it."

"Stunning!" said the marquess. "Tilly? Oh, I see what you mean. Yes, she does rather get on one's nerves with that laugh of hers. Well, we'd better join the guests."

They entered the room and the marquess suddenly stopped rigid. The guests had already witnessed the transformation that was Lady Tilly.

She was wearing a scarlet chiffon dress, as scarlet as her impossible-colored hair. Her creamy shoulders rose from a daringly low neckline. Her white kid gloves were smoothed above her elbows without a wrinkle and the feathers of her large osprey fan fluttered slightly in the cool evening breeze from the garden. Her wide blue eyes stared calmly around the guests and her still childish lips were parted in a tremulous smile. The beautiful ghost that had seemed to flutter before Tilly had suddenly come to life. Be-

hind her, carrying her shawl, stood a smart-
as-paint French maid, neat and demure in a
black silk gown, with her glossy black hair
braided into a coronet.

Then Tilly moved slowly and unhurriedly
into the room as the marquess strode toward
her. There was a little silence. All the guests
waited eagerly, the servants anxiously.
Would she berate her husband for his infidelity?

But Tilly merely held out her gloved hand
and said in her new charming voice, "Philip,
my dear! I trust you did not have too exhausting a journey?"

"I was rather fatigued," said the marquess,
staring at her and wondering if he were having a dream. "But I slept well this afternoon.
Toby tells me he is staying with us for a
while."

"Ah, yes," said the new Tilly, smiling languorously at Toby, who had come up to join
them.

"It's most awfully kind of you to have me,"
said Toby with a strange note in his voice.
The marquess turned slightly in time to catch
the look on his friend's face and frowned. A
new set of thoughts tumbled into his brain.
What the hell had been happening while he

was away? Was this miraculous change in Tilly because of Toby?

He became aware that his wife was addressing him. "I gather you had a most interesting time in Paris," Tilly was saying. "Been studying the flora and fauna, dear?"

"I was on business, as I told you," said the marquess testily.

"So you did," said Tilly lightly and then murmured for his ears alone, "So silly of these newspapers to misinterpret a business trip."

Aileen, too, had noticed the expression on her fiancé's face as he had looked at Tilly, and she quickly masked the rather sour and petulant expression on her own. She may have lost Lord Philip, but Toby Bassett was also a catch. All her girl friends envied her and that meant more to Aileen than any feelings of love or romance.

She moved swiftly forward to take his arm possessively. "I've been asking Toby why he left London," she said with a glittering smile, "but he won't tell poor little me."

"I needed some country air," said Toby, still looking at Tilly. Aileen tightened her grip. "Come, dear," she said in a gentle voice that had, nonetheless, the undertones of pure iron. "Mumsie wants to talk to you."

Toby was led away like a lamb to the slaughter.

Dinner was announced and, moving into the dining room, the marquess had to be content with his wife's company for only that short journey, for he had to take his place at the head of the table, while Tilly seemed to be a mile away at the other end. He became convinced that malice alone had prompted Tilly to seat the Duchess of Glenstraith on his right and Mrs. Barchester, one of the ugliest and most boring women of the county, on his left.

As the dinner progressed he noticed that Tilly seemed to be keeping her end of the table very well amused. Even old Sir Giles Barncaster, a fierce and florid Tory M.P. reputed to loathe all young women, was laughing appreciatively at something she said, and then his voice rang out loud and clear: "Gad, Lady Tilly, but you've got a remarkably well-informed mind!"

Toby's handsome face was leaning too near Tilly's white shoulder.

No one looking at Tilly could even begin to guess at the turmoil of feelings beneath the delectable bosom of her Parisian gown. She had forgotten that her husband was so handsome. Evening dress became him, the stark black and white of its formality setting off his golden head and classic profile. He had acquired a slight tan on his travels, and in a bemused way Tilly noticed, in the blaze of the candelabra, that there was a faint line of gold hair on his cheek.

Aileen was fretting and fuming and wishing she could strangle Toby. She never would have accepted Tilly's cheeky invitation had not her ladyship penciled a note on the bottom of the gilt-edged card informing the Glenstraith family that Toby Bassett was already in residence at Chennington.

Aileen's sour eyes took in the beauty of the formal dining room with its high painted ceilings, its cases gleaming with fine china and silver, and its Adam fireplace. She eyed the well-trained footmen in their splendid livery with a jealous eye. The duchess kept a large staff at her town house in London, but Aileen's newly awakened jealousy saw everything that Tilly had as grander and better. She envied Tilly because Tilly was married and able to wear dashing, bold colors before which she, Aileen, in her palest of pink gowns, faded into insignificance. Aileen, unlike Tilly, had never had to study the art of conversation, for she had considered her beauty enough attraction. Now she had a panicky feeling that all these men around her were actually not listening to her but straining their ears to hear what the fascinating marchioness was saying.

"You know," she said rather loudly to her dinner partner, a young fresh-faced man called Jeremy Beaton, "you'd never guess the poor Beast used to work for me."

"Who?" said Jeremy politely.

"I mean Tilly," said Aileen with that silvery laugh of hers, which eventually grated on the nerves because it always ran up and down exactly the same scale.

"Oh, yes," said Jeremy. "I heard she was your companion before her marriage. Why did you call her 'the Beast'?"

"Because she was so ugly," said Aileen, laughing. "Of course, she's changed a little, but then money and clothes do make a difference."

"Indeed they do," remarked Jeremy in chilling accents. "Lady Tilly is one of the most beautiful women I've ever seen. Why, Toby's quite smitten with her!"

"Toby Bassett is my fiancé!"

"So he is," remarked her companion with infuriating calm. "Sorry. Forgot."

The Duchess of Glenstraith was wishing she had not come. She was wishing she had not let Aileen talk her into organizing the marriage with Bassett. Young Bassett was rich and of good family, but so were a lot of other young men on the London scene. Now she was forced to sit and watch that toad all dressed up in vulgar scarlet queening it from the end of the dinner table. The fact that she, the duchess, took precedence over Tilly in rank was small consolation. Age, as well, went before beauty, so they said. But the only place she would go first would be the grave, as far as Her Grace could see anyway. And there was her husband, quite animated, discussing his latest acquisition—some singularity anemic nudes drawn by Ricketts—to this interloper into the top ten thousand. What did Tilly know of Art Nouveau anyway? Quite a lot, it dawned on the duchess with dismay. She noticed Toby stretching a nervous hand toward his wineglass and gave a loud bark. Toby withdrew the hand instantly and flashed her the sort of look that no dutiful man should give to his future mama-in-law.

The ladies at last retired and, under cover of the general conversation over the port and walnuts, the marquess turned his problem over in his mind. After the way he had treated her, he could hardly tell Tilly that she had to hop into bed with him at the earliest opportunity in order to fulfill the terms of his father's will. Then the thought of hopping into bed with this new and exciting Tilly was infinitely bewitching. The marquess's prowess with women had never been in doubt. He could not see that his wife would prove any exception. He would have to begin to woo her as quickly as possible.

He was impatient to begin his wooing right away and found, to his irritation, that it was going to be harder than he had imagined. His wife suggested a stroll in the gardens, but that invitation seemed to include all the guests.

A full moon silvered the velvet lawns, which seemed to roll off into vast infinity. Heavy roses tumbled and rioted from ironwork trellises and stone urns. The air was heavy with their scent, but the beautiful scene was not made for romance, reflected the marquess wryly, with all these extra characters dotted about.

At last he decided to move into the attack and, extricating himself from the conversational grasp of Mrs. Barchester, he moved forward to the group around his wife and, smiling politely at everyone, gently slid her arm through his own and smiled down at her.

"I have hardly had a chance to exchange a word with you in private since I arrived home," he murmured.

The other guests tactfully began to move away with the exception of Toby Bassett, who stuck like a limpet.

Tilly tried to act calmly, but the pressure of his arm against her own was doing strange things to her breath.

To the marquess's relief the duchess and Aileen closed in on either side of Toby, like jailers, and bore him off.

"Now, Tilly," began the marquess, urging her away from the vicinity of the rest of the guests, "tell the truth. Are you very angry with me?"

"No," lied Tilly calmly. "Why on earth should I be?"

"Because of that report in the newspapers."

"Oh, that. It was true, was it not?" Tilly swung around and looked full into his eyes, and he could not bring himself to lie.

"Yes. I am afraid it was true."

"Well, then," rejoined Tilly brightly, "you did warn me it was more of a business contract than a marriage. You will go your way and I will go mine. And I *am* looking forward to going mine. So many *delicious* young men around!"

He stopped and pulled her to him. "But I don't want you to go in any other direction than this," he whispered.

She opened her mouth to reply with some witty and cynical remark but no sound would come out as she watched his mouth descending, oh so slowly, toward her own in the moonlight. He had removed his gloves and his bare hand was already caressing the nape of her neck. Tilly clutched the lapels of his jacket for support and closed her eyes.

"Your shawl, my lady."

The couple jerked apart. Tilly swung around, flushed and embarrassed. The marquess was furious. Francine stood there demurely in the moonlight with a large white cashmere shawl over her arm.

"The night air, my lady," she went on, ignoring the marquess's glare, "so bad for the lungs."

The marquess dismissed Francine with a curt nod and turned again to his wife. But the treacherous English climate was against him as well. A chilly breeze had sprung up that was strengthening into a full-fledged wind by the second. There were cries of dismay from the ladies, who began scurrying toward the house.

For Tilly, the spell was broken. She was appalled to think that she had been on the point of giving in too easily. Men, the wordly-wise Francine had said, never appreciated anything easy. They walked in silence, side by side, toward the house.

"Where did you get that maid?" asked the marquess.

"From Lady Aileen," said Tilly. "Well, I didn't *get* her, I lured her away, so to speak."

"Funny," he said, looking at her with his fair head cocked to one side, "I could never imagine you concerning yourself with matters of dress."

"Oh, we all have to grow up sometime," Tilly replied lightly.

The guests were organizing themselves for the usual late-evening session of cards. Tilly detested playing cards but hustled her husband into a foursome with the duchess, Lady Aileen, and Toby.

The duchess was a poor cardplayer in that she loudly and obviously suspected everyone of cheating and then kept employing childish ruses like pretending to drop her fan in order to see the marquess's hand. The hair on her face had begun to sprout again, and he found it most unnerving to look down and see her large face coyly peeping over the edge of his arm.

Toby's hands were shaking so badly that his cards fluttered like dry leaves before a desert wind. He eyed the marquess's glass of whisky and soda with burning eyes, as if by some telekinetic means he could suck its contents across the table and into his mouth.

At last the long evening came to an end as the rising wind began to howl around the mansion and the servants moved quietly about with baskets of kindling and scuttles of coal.

The rest of the weary servants heard the bell ringing, a signal that they could put their respective charges to bed and try to catch some much-needed sleep.

Masters rose wearily to his feet and tugged down his striped waistcoat. "I say again," he remarked severely to Francine, "that it is not our place to interfere in the . . . er . . . married lives of our betters."

"I *know* the men, *moi,*" said Francine with such intensity that her listening audience wondered just what her experience had been. "If he gets what he wants on the first night, then *pouf!*—all will be lost. A few days of the

143

honeymoon and then my lord will be off to his amours."

"What on earth can *we* do?" demanded the cook, tucking a strand of gray hair under her cap.

"I'll think of something," was all Francine would say. "Now, I must put my lady to bed . . . *alone.*"

She whisked herself off and Mrs. Judd watched her go with a worried frown. "It's all right for the likes of a Frenchie to talk about them things," she vouchsafed at last. "But I'm a very sensitive person, I am. My sensibilities are *shocked.*"

"She's got a good heart has Francine," said Masters after some deliberation. "Best do as she says."

Upstairs, the marquess tightened the sash of his dressing gown and squared his shoulders. It had seemed a good idea to put his wife's suite of rooms at one end of the West Wing and his own at the other. Now it was simply a damned nuisance. It would be the first time he had crept along the corridor of a country house in the small hours of the morning on legitimate business, so to speak. He stepped out into the dimness of the corridor.

Empty.

Or so he thought. From the shadows at the far end, Toby Bassett watched him go and felt immeasurably sick and depressed. But then, why should not a man spend the night with his own wife?

He realized he had been weaving unreal fantasies about Tilly, forgetting she was married, and to his best friend too.

Then somewhere in the quivering, jellylike hurt of his mind, a little imp seemed to whisper, *"Philip* always *has a decanter in his room. And if* you *were in Tilly's arms, would* you *hurry back?"*

He took a deep breath. The duchess had made sure that his room was innocent of even a flask. He moved quickly down the corridor, feeling as if his life had taken on new hope. He pushed open the door of the marquess's sitting room. There, winking, glistening, and beckoning in the firelight was a full decanter of whisky and standing beside it, like a knight in shining armor, was a glass and a silver siphon of soda. He floated toward it with a rapt expression on his face. His feet hardly seemed to touch the ground.

Also still awake and also in the West Wing, the Duchess of Glenstraith was sitting on her daughter's bed, holding her hand. "So that's it, Mumsie," finished Aileen plaintively. "She's got Philip and now she's taking Toby away from me as well."

"Someone should speak to her husband," said the duchess, hitching the massive folds of her Jaeger dressing gown closer around her flannel nightdress.

"You *must* speak to him," said Aileen, sitting up straight. Her hair was in curlpapers and her face was covered in an oatmeal pack. She looked like a singularly beautiful case of leprosy.

"I shall go to him now, before he retires," said the duchess firmly, "and do my duty."

Aileen blushed under the crust of oatmeal that was hardening rapidly on her pretty face. "Won't he be in . . . well . . . Tilly's room?" she said in as thin a voice as possible so as not to crack the mask.

"No, poppet." The duchess heaved herself to her feet. "Even such a common type as Tilly Burningham wouldn't forgive her husband so soon for his philanderings with that French trollop. Leave it to me."

The marquess paused on the threshold of his wife's room. She was sitting at her dressing table and her maid was brushing her long red hair in smooth, even strokes so that it crackled in the light. The marquess jerked his head to dismiss Francine, but to his amazement the maid showed no signs of leaving and continued to brush her mistress's hair.

He walked forward into the room. "Please leave," he said sharply to Francine, taking the brush from her hand.

"She can't," said Tilly hurriedly. "She has ever such a lot to do here."

The marquess gently eased his wife to her feet and propelled her toward the door. "Then we shall leave her to it," he said. "I wish to be private with you, and my rooms will be the very place."

Tilly opened her mouth to protest. She was wearing a charming nightgown and negligee of creamy slipper satin, no longer protected by her layers of underwear and stays. The sudden awareness that her husband only seemed to be wearing a dressing gown and nothing else stopped her from uttering a word. She was unresistingly led away, only glancing back over her shoulder to catch the worried look on Francine's face.

Halfway along the corridor in the direction of the marquess's rooms, Tilly stopped and turned, trembling slightly. "I have changed my mind," she said firmly. "I wish to go to bed."

"And so you shall," teased the marquess, taking her by the shoulders. He bent and kissed her, holding her closer and closer with an exultant feeling of power as he felt her shudder against him.

Behind his back a door gently opened and Aileen, still wearing her mask, stared in horror at the entwined couple. Tilly must not find her mother waiting in the marquess's rooms! They were so absorbed that she would surely have time to nip quickly along and warn Mumsie.

The duchess was sitting with her large slippered feet on the hearth of the marquess's sitting room when her daughter erupted in, hissing, "They're *both* coming, Mumsie. Tilly mustn't find you here. What excuse could you make?"

Like most of the human race, her grace was a trifle vain of her own appearance. She was sure her presence in the marquess's rooms would mean only one thing to Tilly—that she was having an affair with her husband. The commonsense fact that she was accompanied by a daughter still in curlpapers and an oatmeal mask and could therefore hardly have any designs on the marquess, did not occur to her.

She heard the sound of voices in the corridor and whispered savagely, "Hide! Quick!"

Both women twisted and turned. There were no screens in the room and the curtains were too skimpy to conceal them both. They saw that the inner sitting room door was open to show the bedroom beyond. As one woman, they dived under the great bed—and collided with a chamber pot, a decanter, a siphon of soda . . . and a body. "Shhhhh!" said Toby Bassett's voice from the darkness under the bed. He had gone into hiding at the sound of the duchess's arrival and had subsequently discovered that by dint of twisting his head sideways, he could get his glass to his mouth, and so he had gone to that happy country of the drunk, where even a herd of elephants under his lordship's bed would have failed to disturb his happy euphoria.

But the two ladies had all their senses about them and could hear with painful clarity what was going on in the next room.

"Darling," the marquess murmured, in such a voice that Tilly felt her bones melt and clutched at his shoulders for support, "put your arms round my neck. What are you afraid of?"

"I have this silly feeling that there are people listening," said Tilly.

"Only the birds in the ivy outside," he said, drawing her closer. He began to kiss her languorously and passionately and Tilly moaned against him, failing to hear her moan echoed by the sweating and embarrassed duchess, crammed under the bed with her daughter and a drunk.

His hard lips parted her mouth and his tongue slid between her teeth. Tilly immediately recoiled, backing away from him and scrubbing her mouth with the back of her hand.

"You should not do that!" she cried, while erotic visions of what the marquess might have done flitted through the fevered brains stacked under the bed. "That's . . . that's . . . not *natural*. Who taught you *that?* That French tart?"

The marquess cursed himself. He had forgotten her inexperience.

He had always prided himself on his equable temper, but now he found he was fast losing it. He controlled himself with an effort. "Come and sit here on the sofa by me, Tilly, and let me explain. There are a lot of things you have to learn about the art of making love. . . ."

"There you are," whispered Francine, removing her ear from the door panel. "Too much, too soon. He will frighten her, and she will bore him!"

Mrs. Judd moved away from the door and turned her large and embarrassed face to Masters. "We can't do anything now. It's too late. And it's not *decent,* I tell you, to listen at his lordship's door."

"Never too late," replied Francine. "I have the plan *merveilleux!*" And with that, she flitted silently off down the corridor in the direction of the back stairs.

"So you see," said the marquess, after a lengthy lecture on the arts of love, of which Tilly understood not a word, "it is all very simple." He drew Tilly into the circle of his arms and, sliding his arms under her legs, prepared to carry her off to bed.

Tilly looked at him helplessly with a drowned expression in her eyes. She had no longer any power to resist him. Although she had not understood his lecture, the sound of his voice had a hypnotic charm all of its own. The marquess carried her into the bedroom and stood looking down at her lovingly as he prepared to lower her onto the bed.

And then the fire alarm went. It clanged and crashed its brazen warning. And what a tale of terror did its turbulency tell to the listeners under the bed. The duchess and Aileen bolted forth like rocketing pheasants. Fortunately for them, the marquess had dropped Tilly on the bed and had rushed to open the window, not seeing who was fleeing his room. Tilly only saw Aileen's leprous masked face and, convinced it was some hideous ghost of Chennington, screwed her eyes shut and screamed.

Toby Bassett was the only one unconcerned. He had fallen into a deep and peaceful sleep.

Soon, with the exception of Toby, all the guests and servants were huddled out on the lawn in the chill predawn air, staring up at the great mansion, waiting for a sign of smoke or flames.

Suddenly there was a united gasp as the windows on the front of the house burned red and the shout went up for buckets of water and everyone began to run hither and thither, screaming confusing orders.

It was some time before it was discovered that the sinister red light on the windows was merely that of the rising sun.

It took a little more time to discover there was no fire at all.

Francine tenderly shepherded her mistress

off to bed. "Saved by the bell!" she murmured. There would be time enough to lecture Tilly after she, Francine, had had some
well-earned sleep.

CHAPTER SEVEN

Tilly sat up in bed late the next morning, sipping her tea and munching Osborne biscuits, while Francine straightened out the rows of jars and scent bottles on the dressing table.

Rain pattered against the windows and a cheerful fire crackling on the hearth combated the chill of this unusually cold summer's day.

"Now," said Francine, stepping back and surveying the dressing table, "it is time for the lecture."

"Rats!" said Tilly grumpily, looking remarkably like a slimmer version of her old self.

Undeterred, Francine drew up a chair beside the bed and sat down. "Lady Tilly," she began, "you must tell me exactly what happened last night."

"I don't see that it's any of your business," said Tilly sulkily. "I'm not a child."

"You are an innocent when it comes to the art of lovemaking," replied Francine.

"Well, it was all right until you started ringing that bell," said Tilly huffily.

"And nothing happened to startle you or embarrass you?"

"Yes, well, there was something," said Tilly, blushing.

"Then tell me, my lady, and I will help. I do not believe in this custom of keeping young girls in ignorance. I remember my own experience . . ." She paused, bit her lip, and then laughed. "But that, as your Rudyard Kipling would say, is another story. Tell me yours."

Tilly hung her head, but the desire to confide was too much for her and, eventually, in halting tones, she told Francine of that strange kiss that had so repelled her, so attracted her at the same time.

Francine tried not to smile. Her mistress was an innocent indeed!

"It is quite usual," she said. "One does not always simply purse up one's lips, so . . . for the kiss. Which brings me to the main point. The marquess is a very experienced man, my lady. If you fall into his arms like the ripe

156

fruit, it will all be too easy, and then perhaps he will return to Paris to seek his amours."

"I know . . . these women exist," sighed Tilly. "But they cannot surely compete with true love."

"Ah, yes, they can. Some of the highest courtesans in France have been training since birth for their roles. They are witty and clever and never dull. Why do you think I made you read all those books and newspapers and go through so many rehearsals? You must keep him at arm's length, just a little longer."

"It seems so very hard," said Tilly, climbing out of bed. "I mean, playing all these games when all I really want to do is send everyone away and be alone with him."

"That will come," reassured the lady's maid. "For this evening, you must plead the fatigue. In fact, you do look a little pale."

"Oh, that's something else," wailed Tilly. "How could I forget. Oh, Francine. We've a *ghost* at Chennington!"

The lady's maid crossed herself. "Where did you see this apparition?"

Tilly explained about the horrible face that had looked back at her after the fire bell rang.

Francine's voice dropped to a whisper. "And did it slide through the door?" she asked in an awed voice.

"No, it didn't," said Tilly, wrinkling her brow with the effort of memory. "Philip heard the bell and dropped me on the bed and ran to the window. And these two . . . *things* . . . came out from under the bed—the room was half dark, you know—and then the awful one turned in the doorway and . . . and . . . then, it went out and slammed the door behind it!"

"There you are. It could not be a phantom. Did my lord see it?"

"No. He had his head out of the window. But no human could have such an awful face."

"I have the plan," said Francine briskly. "I will help you dress and then I will run along to your husband's rooms, and if he has quitted them, I will come back for you and we will search for the evidence—just like Scotland Yard!"

Tilly reluctantly agreed. Soon she was dressed and soon Francine returned with the news that "my lord" had gone off to visit one of the tenants.

The two girls entered the marquess's rooms and looked around nervously. The curtains had been drawn back, but the day was dark and the ivy outside tapped against the pane in a truly gothic manner.

They tiptoed into the bedroom and with a quick look at one another, knelt down on the floor. Francine slowly lifted the bedcovers up and both peered underneath. A deep snore came from a huddled black shape against the far wall. Tilly opened her mouth to scream, but Francine put her hand over Tilly's mouth and whispered, "Ghosts do not snore. Fetch the lamp."

With trembling fingers they lit the lamp and peered under the bed. Toby Bassett was revealed, deep in blissful sleep. The smell of stale whisky was appalling. An empty whisky decanter lay on its side on the floor.

"Monsieur!" called Francine in a sharp voice. Toby sat up and banged his head on the underside of the bed. He rolled over on his side and stared at the two women, then he rolled back and stared up at the bed. "Where am I?" he said at last in a faint voice.

"You are under Monsieur le Marquis's bed," said Francine patiently.

Toby groaned and rolled over and over until he lay at their feet, blinking his eyes in the light. He groaned and put his hand to his forehead. "I remember now," he said. "I wanted to pinch some of Philip's whisky and I saw him going off to Tilly's rooms. So I crept into the sitting room and was just enjoying myself no end when I heard someone coming to the door. I took the whisky and doings and dived under the bed. Well, who should I see when I looked out but that great fat thing of a duchess, sitting in front of the fire.

"Then, next thing, her daughter comes rushing in and they both dive under the bed and nearly smother me. I think it was her daughter, except her face was all scaly. So I went to sleep. Couldn't stand the sight of them," he added casually, forgetting that his beloved fiancée was one of the two women to whom he was referring. "Don't tell Philip. He'd murder me."

Tilly had recovered from her fright, relieved to learn that the mansion was not haunted after all. She helped Francine raise the shaky Toby to his feet, reflecting that he was one of the few men who became improved by a hangover. His tousled locks fell romantically over his pale forehead and his dark eyes burned with a seemingly romantic fire. Toby groaned again and buried his head in his hands. "I will go and fetch the sal volatile," said Francine, departing swiftly and leaving the door open.

"I won't wait," said Toby, struggling to his

feet. "Must get a bath and a change of clothes. Can't be found like this."

He staggered and clutched hold of Tilly, who supported him to the door. "Please don't tell Philip," pleaded Toby. "He'd think it was a bit much. I mean, passing out under his bed."

"I won't," promised Tilly.

"Philip's a lucky man," said Toby, suddenly focussing on the heart-shaped face turned up to his own. He bent and kissed her on the cheek.

"What the *hell* is going on here?" demanded the Marquess of Heppleford from the doorway.

Tilly blushed guiltily. "Toby just dropped by to see if there was any sal volatile," she lied.

"Must go," said Toby and bolted from the room. The marquess eyed his wife. He was amazed at his own feeling of fury at seeing Tilly in Toby's arms. He remembered that quite a lot of women found Toby attractive. He, the marquess, had felt invulnerable up till that minute, encased in the armor of his own good looks. Now he began to doubt their power to charm.

"What are you doing in my rooms?" he demanded harshly.

"Looking for you," said Tilly calmly, although her heart was hammering against her ribs.

He closed the door behind him and locked it. "That is what I like to hear," he said, moving slowly toward her. "It was time you came looking for me."

Tilly opened her mouth to say she hadn't come looking for him and then remembered her promise to Toby. Francine, listening in the corridor outside, fled. Action must be taken quickly. It was too soon!

"Why was Toby kissing you?" demanded the marquess, catching her hand and drawing her against him.

"It was a brotherly kiss," said Tilly, breathlessly. "He had been drinking last night and felt awful, and I was just being sympathetic."

"Well, in the future, you will be sympathetic to no one but me," said the marquess, tracing the line of her cheekbone with his finger.

Tilly could feel her treacherous body beginning to tremble against his and made a last stand. "What about our contract?" she cried. "We weren't going to meddle in each other's affairs. What about that woman in Paris?"

"I must have been mad," said the marquess. "I did not realize I had all this here.

You have grown very quickly into an enchant-ing woman. Kiss me, Tilly."

Still, she turned her head away. "It's too easy," she whispered. "When you're tired of me, you'll go looking for another mistress."

"No," he said slowly. "I don't think I will. You must trust me, Tilly." He put his hand under her chin and forced her to look at him. She stared up into those eyes as deep and as blue as her own and knew that she was help-less. His hand was loosening the bone pins that secured her hair and it came tumbling about her shoulders in a red cascade.

"Kiss me, Tilly," he urged, winding his hand in the tumble of her hair. "Kiss me . . . now."

She closed her eyes, feeling the now famil-iar hard lips against her own, searching and probing. The little sounds of the outside world penetrated for a few moments: the sound of the birds squabbling in the ivy; the patter of rain against the window; a servant somewhere along the corridor, whistling as he went about his work; and then all sight and sound went spinning away as she became more deeply enclosed in a dark world of pas-sion, where nothing existed but the feel of his long fingers and the pressure of his lips.

Crrrump! Like an exploding bomb, a brick

hurtled down into the remains of last night's fire, sending a huge, suffocating cloud of ash and soot swirling around them. They fell apart, choking and gasping, and then Tilly ran to tug open the window while the marquess rang the bell and unlocked the door. To his surprise, a bevy of footmen almost fell into the room. The marquess's feelings were suddenly as black and suspicious as his soot-streaked face. He prided himself on the efficiency of his servants, but it did seem odd that so many should answer the summons of the bell when he hadn't even called for help and could have been ringing for his shaving water.

The marquess and Tilly looked a sorry pair. Both were covered in black soot and ash from head to foot. Both were suffering from the dizzying effects of shock and interrupted passion.

When Masters arrived to announce that Cyril Nettleford, his lordship's nephew, was waiting belowstairs, the marquess's wrath knew no bounds.

"What in hell and damnation is going on in this house?" he roared. "First some fool rings the alarm bell when there's no fire, then someone throws a brick down the chimney, and now that unmitigated ass, Cyril, is camped out in my drawing room. Tell him to leave, Masters!"

"I am afraid I cannot do that," said Masters. "You have always welcomed any of your relatives before this, my lord, and you have not issued any orders to the contrary. Mr. Nettleford has been accommodated in the Blue Room, my lord, and his hired carriage has been sent back to London."

"Of all the—" began the marquess, but Tilly placed a soothing hand on his arm. "I shall have a quick bath, Philip, and see if I can get rid of him." And before he could reply, she was gone.

Cyril Nettleford waited impatiently in the drawing room. It was not the lord he wanted to see but the lady. He had seen the Beast on her wedding day and, knowing the terms of the old marquess's later will, had been delighted. He had been ecstatic at the news from Paris. Philip would never beget a legitimate heir, the way he was carrying on. And he, Cyril, stood to inherit the marquess's fortune if no heir were forthcoming. But he had also learned at the wedding that the marquess had not known of the later will. A visit to the family solicitors then revealed that the marquess now *did* know and was quite prepared to do something about it. Cyril had arrived at Chennington to see if there was anything he could do to put a spoke in the married couple's life. He was sure there would have been no reconciliation at this early date (for what wife would not be furious at her husband spending his wedding night in the arms of a French tart?), but he wanted to make sure there would *never* be one.

His heart sank as Tilly was announced. What the *hell* had happened to the Beast? A slim redhead, dressed in a saucy tailored skirt and striped blouse, stood before him. Her eyes were wide and a dazzling blue and not the little crinkled slits he had remembered. And her hair was no longer frizzed, but twisted and coiled by the hand of a genius. She was wearing some faint and elusive perfume that was seduction itself. How on earth was Philip going to keep his hands off her?

Tilly was equally amazed at what she saw. She thought Mr. Nettleford looked like a species of spotted snake. He had lank fair hair and lank Piccadilly weepers growing down either side of his face. His face had a greenish tinge that was marred by clumps of angry red spots, and his eyes were green and slightly protruding. He wore the latest thing in double-breasted suits and his spats gleamed as whitely as the tops of Beau Brummell's riding

166

boots no doubt used to gleam across the spinneys and fields of Regency England.

"So kind of you to invite me," he said, rising to his feet.

Tilly decided it was time to deliver the cut direct. "I rather gather you invited yourself, Mr. Nettleford, and as we already have a houseful of guests . . ." She let her voice delicately trail away, but Mr. Nettleford had been snubbed by experts. "Oh, good," he cried. "Obviously you mean that with so many guests, what difference does another one make. Ha, ha, ha."

Tilly winced. She knew that when people laughed in books it was written down as "Ha, ha, ha," but never before had she heard someone who actually laughed like that.

Tilly was about to persevere in her attempt to get rid of him, but the wily Cyril guessed so before she opened her mouth and counteracted by changing the subject—dramatically.

"You must have been amazed at the terms of my great uncle's will, Lady Tilly. I mean the *second* will."

"Really?" Tilly raised her eyebrows in the haughtiest manner possible. "I certainly found the will, but I did not read it. It is my husband's business, after all. Don't you find it so irritating, Mr. Nettleford, when people poke their noses into what does not concern them?"

Cyril flushed but recovered quickly. "Oh, you really should ask your husband about that will," he murmured. "After all, it does concern you as much as he."

Tilly weighed into the attack. "We are expecting more guests, Mr. Nettleford. I really must ask you to leave, since you were not invited and your rooms will be needed for the *invited* guests as soon as they arrive."

"Oh, indeed!" agreed Cyril with an unlovely smile. "And as soon as they *do* arrive, I shall, of course, move out."

Tilly bit her lip in vexation. Well, the least she could do was to make his stay as uncomfortable as possible.

"I shall see that you are served tea, Mr. Nettleford," she said. "And I shall send one of our guests to see you. No! No! You mustn't spoil my surprise. It is someone who is *dying* to meet you!"

And with that, Tilly went in search of the Duchess of Glenstraith and told that astounded woman that Mr. Cyril Nettleford was a hardened drinker and in need of spiritual guidance. The duchess let out a war cry and descended on the drawing room, where the unfortunate Cyril, who had settled for the whisky decanter rather than tea, was subjected to one of the longest and most boring lectures he had ever endured in his life.

The day passed, wet and miserable, and the guests pottered about in that half-awake bored and boring way they usually do when there is nothing to do but eat and drink.

The marquess kept looking for his wife and finding her unaccountably absent, as Tilly was holding a council of war in the servants' quarters. "You have all been very kind," she was saying firmly, "but it has got to stop. I think things should be left to take their natural course."

"Well, if you say so, my lady," said Masters anxiously. "We certainly didn't think it natural to interfere between husband and wife, but Miss Francine was so set on it."

"And I still am," said Francine. "I wish to speak to you in private, Lady Tilly."

Both women retired to one of the unused rooms in the East Wing and Tilly rounded on Francine. "I can't hold out any longer," she cried. "I'll lose him. What do you know of it? *You* aren't married."

Francine gave a heavy sigh and looked at her hands. *"Eh bien,"* she said at last. "I will tell you my story. I was in service in this château in France. Milord was very, very handsome and milady was ailing. Milord was always teasing me and flirting with me. One day he told me that his love for me was real, that he would marry me as soon as his wife died. I believed him. I never thought of his wife. We are careless and selfish when we are so in love. That night, he came to my room. He was a marvelous lover, tender and experienced. We had a rapturous seven days. *Seven days,* that is all, my lady. Then his wife talked to me. She told me sadly that she knew what was going on and that she was sorry for me, because I was obviously in love with her husband. 'He is merely amusing himself,' she told me. 'He will forget you when the next one comes along.'

"I thought she was jealous. That night, we had a grand ball at the château and I had to watch milord flirting with one of the *grande* ladies. My heart was sore, but still I thought he loved me. I hid behind the screen in his rooms that night—he did not sleep with milady—waiting for him to come to bed. Which he did—with the new amour—and I was trapped there, listening. It was horrible! You see, I thought my love would change him. But people do not change, my lady, and certainly not men who are used to a series of amours. If I had remained aloof, virginal, I would have kept him for quite a time. But as it was—"

"No," said Tilly, her face hardening. "It's not the same. I know it's not. He's just not used to being married, that's all. And he wants *me,* Francine. Me! Out of all the girls in the world. Oh, I know it's because of the marvelous change you've made in me, Francine, but there's still the old Tilly underneath and *that* is what he loves. I know he loves me. I can see it in his eyes. So no more interference, Francine."

Francine raised her hands in mute protest, but Tilly swung on her heels and marched from the room.

CHAPTER EIGHT

The marquess had taken pity on his bored guests and had organized an impromptu entertainment for them that evening, arranging a ball to be held in the upper chain of salons. He had hired a band from the neighboring town for the occasion.

The old mansion came alive with rustling, scurrying, and whispering as the old magic of a ball took hold of the guests. Aileen decided to forgive Toby. Toby decided to go on pretending that he was going to marry Aileen when he was sure that he was not. Cyril Nettleford twisted and turned in front of the mirror, admiring his reflection and thinking that he could perhaps woo Tilly away from her husband. The Duchess of Glenstraith sang in her bath in a loud bass voice as she considered the joys of reclaiming Cyril Nettleford's soul, and even her husband tum-tummed happily from the next room as he studied an art catalog.

Tilly and Francine examined one ball gown after the other, searching for one that would look the most romantic. Francine had shrugged and capitulated and had decided to make Tilly look as breathtaking as possible.

The only gloomy member of the house party was the marquess himself. The nagging guilt he had felt over his behavior on his wedding night had become a monumental ache. He tried to think of the old Tilly, rough, noisy, and uncouth and tried hard not to blame himself. He would *make* her love him, he decided at last, and then everything would be all right. He never stopped to consider whether he was in love with her himself. She was his wife, after all!

Soon the strains of the inevitable waltz could be heard drifting through the house as the musicians rehearsed. Soon the carpets were rolled up and Masters gave an approving nod of his head at the gleaming floors. Great tubs of flowers were carried in from the hothouse and banked against the walls.

Tilly was wearing a daringly low-cut dress of white silk chiffon, swathed over her bosom to mold her breasts and pulled tight at the waist to accentuate her hourglass figure. Her husband had sent her a long box containing the Heppleford diamonds, beautifully cleaned and reset. Even Francine was awed into silence as she clasped the heavy gems around Tilly's neck and secured the blazing tiara in Tilly's hair, where it seemed to catch fire from the vivid red color and blazed and sparkled.

As she was prepared to leave, Francine gave a final tweak to Tilly's curls and then kissed her gently on the cheek. "Be careful," she whispered.

Tilly laughed. She was young, she was in love, and she was married to the most handsome man in the world.

Lord Philip, Marquess of Heppleford, watched his wife walk into the ballroom, his eyes glowing with admiration. She looked magnificent. He was overcome with tenderness and admiration for the lumpy schoolgirl who had managed to transform herself into a woman who turned all men's heads. He was not aware of Cyril Nettleford watching him narrowly from the corner. Cyril's stomach felt as if it had just experienced a journey in a very fast-moving lift, especially as he noticed that the marquess's gaze was returned by a warm and glowing one from his wife. It was then he remembered the copy of the second will that he had obtained from the solicitors and which was now reposing among his luggage upstairs.

Tilly's newfound confidence and happiness leant wings to her feet. She seemed to float over the floor, laughing and chatting with her partners, her little dance card swinging from her wrist, full of names.

Aileen, who was looking like the fairy her mother called her in silver and white gauze, laughed and chattered and quite charmed her reluctant fiancé. Even the Duchess of Glenstraith shook the floor in a lively set of the lancers, while her reedy husband pirouetted around her like some Don Quixote about to tilt at a particularly lively windmill.

Finally Tilly was in her husband's arms, moving dreamily through the long rooms to the sound of a waltz, under the flickering flames of hundreds of candles, since the marquess considered old-fashioned lighting more suitable for a ball. Watching from the doorway, Masters heaved a sentimental sigh. My lord and my lady were obviously very much in love. He should never have listened to Miss Francine, not that mademoiselle didn't have her mistress's interests at heart, but then how could a foreigner judge the heart of an Englishwoman? Ecstatic with happiness, Masters smiled on his master and mistress as they glided past him in each others arms. They danced at regulation fingertip distance, but they might have been clasped close together from the expression in their eyes.

All Tilly's past humiliations vanished. She could even find it in her to smile on Aileen and the duchess.

At long last, after the supper was over and after a few more dances, the visiting guests went home, the lights of their carriages bobbing off down the long drive. The weary house guests took themselves off to bed.

Tilly smiled up at her husband, suddenly shy. He bent and kissed her lightly on the cheek. "Tonight," he whispered, and she nodded mutely. "I will see you in your rooms presently," he murmured. "I will not be long."

As Tilly sat in front of her dressing table, Francine brushed out her long red hair and arranged the lacy folds of her negligee. She turned down the lamps, all except one in the sitting room and one in the bedroom, and formally curtsied and left.

Tilly was suddenly very nervous. Should she sit on a chair and wait for him? Should she climb into bed? She eventually decided to sit up in bed with a book and read until he appeared.

The gentle sound of the door opening made her heart beat faster. She looked up at him as he approached the bed with her heart in her eyes. He was wrapped in his dressing gown and his fair hair was still damp from the bath. He sat down on the edge of the bed and gave her a heartrending smile. "Love me, Tilly?" he asked.

"I don't know," said Tilly shyly. She wanted to say she loved him more than anything in the world, but a little cynical voice in her brain seemed to be crying caution.

"Then I shall make you love me," he said, smiling. He stood up and removed his dressing gown, and Tilly quickly averted her eyes from his naked body. He lifted the bedclothes and climbed in beside her, his long, hard muscular body pressing against her own. Tilly experienced a terrible spasm of fear and unreality. And then his mouth came down on hers, almost savagely, and each long, hard kiss seemed to take the fear away, bit by bit, until she could feel nothing but aching, overwhelming passion.

Then she realized he was asking her something, his voice seeming to come from very

178

far away. She struggled to the surface of the sea of passion. "What?"

"That damned crackling sound," he said, propping himself up on his elbows and leaning over her. "Have you got newspapers or something under your pillows?"

"No!" said Tilly, startled. "At least I don't think so." She twisted around and felt under the pillow with her hand, drawing out a long folded piece of parchment. "It's that will!" said Tilly in amazement. "No, it's a copy, a copy of your father's will. What on earth is it doing here?"

But the marquess was laughing. "You sly puss," he said. "You knew the terms of the second will after all." He wrapped his arms around her. "Well, my papa never guessed what a pleasant duty making an heir could be."

Tilly went rigid in his arms. "What if you don't produce an heir?" she asked faintly.

"Oh, *you* know," said her husband, laughing. "The first will said I had to marry to inherit, and the second said that not only had I to marry, but to produce an heir as well. Isn't it rich? My papa was more eccentric than I had imagined. He was so keen on keeping on the direct line. What's wrong, Tilly?"

Tilly sat bolt upright in bed and gave him

a violent push. "Don't touch me!" she gasped. "You don't l-love m-me at all. You're only obeying your father's will. This is nothing more than another business contract. Oh, God, I'm so ashamed."

"Don't be a ninny," said the marquess, trying to take her in his arms. "You love me, don't you?"

With that last sentence the marquess proved he was not the expert lover, the Don Juan he had fondly believed himself to be. Had he said "I love you," Tilly might have forgiven him. But as it was, she crouched up against the bedhead and glared at him with the savagery of a wildcat.

"Get out!" she yelled. "OUT! OUT! OUT!"

"Now, look, my dear," began her husband, trying to be reasonable and finding it to be rather difficult while stark naked. But Tilly's next remark stopped him short. She had been feverishly searching her mind for something to say that would hurt him as much as he had hurt her. Suddenly changing her voice to calm, measured tones, she faced him. "It would not have worked anyway," she said. "After all, I am inexperienced in the arts of love . . . and I could only go on pretending

180

you were Toby Bassett to make it all sufferable for a certain length of time."

"Toby! Are you trying to tell me you are in love with Toby?"

"Yes, only I'm married to you, so I thought I ought to try to make the best of it."

"You thought—why, you naive little cat. You're trying to make me jealous!"

"I only wish I were," said Tilly sadly, her hurt driving her to acting heights she had never guessed she possessed. She began to cry, "Oh, Toby, if only you loved me!"

To the appalled marquess it had the terrible ring of conviction. He did not know that all Tilly had wanted to do was utter the heartfelt cry of, "Oh, Philip, if only you loved me."

He stood up and shrugged into his dressing gown.

"I bid you good night, madam," he said, glaring down at the sobbing figure on the bed.

Tilly raised her tearstained face. "I suppose you'll be rushing off to that trollop in Paris."

"An excellent idea," he grated.

"You know your trouble," said Tilly, hitting wildly on the truth, "your trouble is, you can't recognize genuine love, because you've only paid for it or found it in some bored married woman's arms."

There is nothing more devastating than the truth.

The marquess slapped his marchioness full across the face.

Tilly's anguish fled before an overmastering burst of rage.

"You cad, sir!" she cried. "You unutterable *bounder.*"

And with that she punched the marquess full on the end of his aristocratic nose.

Before he could recover from that attack, Tilly had flown to the marble washstand and, picking up the copper jug, emptied the contents over his head.

He turned abruptly on his heel and slammed his way out of the room.

Tilly threw herself facedown on the bed and cried her eyes out.

Only when the birds began to stir in the ivy outside and a bright sun rose over the horizon, heralding the beginning of a beautiful day, did she fall into an exhausted sleep.

The first thought she had on awakening some hours later was that Francine had gone too far. Tilly was in no doubt that the lady's maid had somehow known about the contents of the will and had placed the copy under her pillow. The marchioness sat up in bed and grimly rang the bell.

But Francine's surprise and dismay were all too genuine. The other servants were called in and questioned and all were vehement in their denials. It was then that Tilly remembered Cyril Nettleford and his hints about the will.

"Let me see the will," said Francine. She bent her head and read it carefully. "But it is evident, my lady," she cried. "It says here quite plainly that if my lord does not produce an heir, then Cyril Nettleford will inherit. And furthermore, my lady, I watched his lordship last night and he looked to me like a man very much in love, and I said to myself that I have made the mistake regarding him."

"I told him I was in love with Toby," wailed Tilly. "But it was his own fault. Why didn't he tell me about the will?"

"I think he would have done—eventually," said Francine. "After all, he seemed to feel guilty about his behavior after the wedding, so it follows that he could not immediately come home and ask you coldly to fulfill the terms of his father's will, now could he?"

"I suppose not," said Tilly reluctantly. "Oh, he won't want to *look* at me again after last night. I—I punched him on the nose and threw water over him."

Francine bit her lip to suppress a smile. "You must go on as if nothing has happened. Visit your tenants. It is your duty to see them."

"I don't think they'd really like that," said Tilly, remembering Mrs. Pomfret. "I was always poking my nose in at Jeebles and keeping them off their work."

"But you shall only drop in, say, for a few minutes. Just to shake the hand, *non?*" said Francine. "And we will get rid of our house guests."

But the house guests proved to be hard to dislodge. The more sensitive souls admittedly took the well-worn hint presented to them in the form of the railway timetable laid on their bedside tables, with the fastest and soonest train underlined in red ink, but the ducal family Glenstraight clung on, as did Toby Bassett and Cyril Nettleford. During the next three days, the marquess was mostly absent, only returning very late at night. He did not look at or talk to Tilly. He certainly snubbed his friend Toby on every occasion, which went completely unnoticed by that gentleman, since he was now in his usual state of semioblivion.

It was only during one of his rare periods of sobriety that it finally penetrated Mr. Bassett's well-soaked hide that his friend, Philip, was looking daggers at him.

"Why are you looking at me like that?" asked Toby plaintively.

"I'm looking at you like 'that' because you're a bloody snake in the grass," snapped the marquess. "And I wish you'd toddle off home and stop philandering with my wife."

"Philandering with—I say, you're talking rubbish. What about a drink, Philip? The sun's over the yardarm."

"The sun's barely over the anchor chain, you unmitigated twit. Leave my wife alone or I'll knock your head off."

"I haven't touched her," complained Toby, trying to concentrate on what the marquess was saying. "Look, old man, we've been friends for years. Explain the whole thing, but slowly. My head's in not too good a shape."

"Very well," said the marquess coldly, finally reciting what Tilly had said after the finding of the will.

"Who put it there?" asked Toby simply.

"What?"

"I said, 'Who put it there?'" repeated Toby patiently. "Someone put it there to make trouble."

The marquess stared at his friend for a long minute. Then he said slowly, "Of course, *she* could have put it there to pick a fight with me. Dear God, d'you know what she said? She, Tilly, my wife, said that she was in love with you and that the only way she could endure my lovemaking was to pretend I was *you.*"

"Tell you what," said Toby wildly, "I'm not asking you for a drink, I'm ordering one!"

"I'll join you," said the marquess gloomily.

Toby ordered brandy, "for shock, you know" and poured a sizable amount down his throat. Another few thousand brain cells hit the dust, but the survivors were galvanized into feverish action.

"It's all very strange," said Toby, frowning horribly under the pressure of all this unaccustomed thought. "I made Tilly promise not to tell you, because I felt such an ass, but here goes."

He told the amazed marquess of hiding under the bed with the duchess and Lady Aileen. "For heaven's sake!" cried the marquess, "you're all turning my marriage into some sort of French farce."

"I thought you were doing that pretty well yourself," said Toby with rare nastiness, and before his friend could reply, he hurriedly went on. "Has it dawned on you that we haven't thought of Cyril Nettleford? *He's* the one who stands to inherit if you don't produce an heir."

"Of course!" The marquess put down his glass. "That's it! He always was a nasty piece of work. You remember that scandal with the Quennell's footman? But, laddie, that still does not explain my wife's sudden passion for you. Tilly's a good girl, for all her nonsense, and she wouldn't say anything like that if it weren't true."

"I had a bit of a crush on Tilly," said Toby while his friend scowled horribly, "but I got over it. And I'll tell you how I got over it, apart from drinking whisky under your bed. I saw that Tilly was head over heels in love with you."

"Then why would she . . . ?"

"Hurt," said Toby, who like most habitual drunks was an expert on the subject. "Thought you were only romanticating her cos you needed an heir. So she says the first thing she can think of to hurt you. But she ain't in love with me. Wish she were."

"I thought you were over it?"

"I am. I am. But, I mean, compare Tilly with my fiancée. Not in the same league. Tilly's all fire, and Aileen's all milk and water and bitchiness. Pity. She looks like an angel."

"So," said the marquess, ticking the points off on his fingers. "Tilly is in love with me. She said those things about you to hurt me. Nettleford put the will under her pillow because he had found out somehow that she didn't know the terms. Fine. Now we come to the other unanswered question. What were Her Grace and your fiancée doing under my bed? If that alarm bell hadn't rung, you'd all have been there listening. . . . It doesn't bear thinking of."

But Toby's powers of concentration had worn out. Nonetheless, he made one last effort. "If you want to know what the duchess was doing under your bed," he said, in a lazy, slurred voice, "then you'd better ask her."

The marquess, whistling, went off in search of Her Grace.

He felt immeasurably more cheerful. The duchess, when he questioned her, was sulky and defiant. She had been about to talk to him for his own good and had waited in his rooms, not dreaming *for a minute* that he would . . . er . . . visit his wife so soon after that Paris episode. Anyway, Aileen had come to warn her and she and her daughter had hidden under the bed.

Why?

The duchess turned puce. Well, if Lord Philip would face facts, she was still . . . harrumph . . . an attractive woman and Tilly might have suspected the worst.

The marquess stared at Her Grace in amazement, reflecting that many supposed do-gooders seemed to have absolute sewers for minds.

"Anyway," pursued Her Grace, "I may as well tell you now what I meant to tell you then. You've got to tell that wife of yours to lay off Toby. She's a bad influence, and the poor chap has taken to the bottle again. She even tried to throw me off the track by setting me on that repulsive Nettleford fellah."

"Are you trying to tell me that Tilly has been making advances to Mr. Bassett?" asked the marquess stiffly.

"Well, no," said the duchess fairly. "But she's getting herself up like a tart, encouraged by that brassy maid, Francine. She took Francine away from my fairy and now she's going to take her fiancé away as well."

"Piffle," said the marquess rudely. "You got Toby when he was drunk, the pair of you. You don't want it spread around London that Lady Aileen can't get married unless she tricks some poor chap into it."

"And who would spread about such a malicious and *untrue* piece of gossip?"

"Me," said the marquess cheerfully and ungrammatically. He was not in the least afraid of the formidable duchess.

"I should never have brought my fairy to this sink of iniquity," raged the duchess. "You can tell that Bassett fellah the engagement is *off!*"

As if on cue, Aileen sailed in to be told the news, which she received with surprising calm. "I am glad you have settled this for me. I know the news will break poor Toby's heart," she said, "but I cannot spend the rest of my life with a drunk."

"I shall tell the servants you are leaving immediately," said the marquess coldly. He had a sudden feeling of compassion for his wife. How on earth had she endured this terrible couple?

Tilly was gladdened some two hours later by the sight of the Glenstraith's traveling carriage lumbering off down the drive with a mountain of luggage balanced precariously on the roof.

Toby Bassett also watched the departure. He was glad he would not have to endure any more lectures from the duchess.

The sun was blazing down on the heavy summer green of the countryside. The lawns stretched out to the lake like fields of green glass and each heavy rose hanging in the still hot air seemed to have been formed from the finest porcelain. Tilly stretched up her arms in relief. Now if only Cyril Nettleford would leave.

CHAPTER NINE

Tilly sat under the cool trees of the vicarage garden and looked about her with pleasure. Variegated lupins blazed against the old red brick of the garden wall and a moss-covered sundial at the edge of the shaggy lawn marked off the passage of the sunny hours with one long, shadowy finger.

She was making the first of her social calls, accompanied by the ever-correct Francine. She had not seen her husband and had felt too nervous and shy after the scene of *that night* to go in search of him.

The vicar was a small, plump, scholarly man called Mr. Waring. His tight-fitting clericals were shiny with age, but his round, gentle face gave him a pleasing dignity. His wife was younger than he and pretty, in a faded-blond way, with silver threads in her fair hair and faded-blue eyes. Witness to what must have once been her undoubted beauty was there in the presence of her daughter, Emily, a pretty, lively girl with rosy country cheeks and thick fair hair piled up over a wide forehead.

Mr. Waring was mourning the death of one of his parishoners," . . . a wild fellow and as strong as an ox until the drink got to him."

Tilly remembered Toby's family failing. "Is there no cure?" she asked. "Surely it is a matter of willpower. Can't one just stop? It is a moral weakness, after all."

"I do not understand it, my dear," said the vicar gently. "Sometimes a strong belief in God effects a cure. That is my department. Sometimes just a belief in something or someone *outside* themselves. I have seen rips of fellows cured after they've fallen in love with pretty girls."

Tilly glanced speculatively at the pretty face of Emily Waring. But did Toby ever sober up enough to notice a pretty face?

The vicar and his wife began to talk of parish matters, while Emily played with a shaggy puppy in the grass. Tilly watched her. *She must be only a year younger than me,* she thought, *and yet she romps away there without looking like a tomboy. Perhaps one day*

194

I can work backward from all these rigid social manners and social conventions.

Suddenly a picture of her husband's lean, hard naked body danced before her eyes, and she felt quite dizzy and faint. This could not be love, thought Tilly angrily. It was more like a sickness.

Then a shadow fell across her and she looked up into the blue eyes of the cause of her sickness and her heart did several somersaults.

He did not look at all angry, she noticed when she could. He was smiling at her, actually smiling.

The marquess drew up a garden chair next to the vicar and began to chat in his light, pleasant voice.

"Who is that gorgeously romantic man?" whispered Emily.

"My husband," said Tilly, with pride.

"No," whispered Emily shyly, "not his lordship. That young man over there."

Tilly turned her head. Toby Bassett was standing at the garden gate. His face was as pale as marble and his eyes smoldered as he looked across at the group. *Really,* thought Tilly, *if one didn't know Toby was drunk, one would think he was in the throes of compos-*

ing an epic. But she merely said, "It is my husband's friend Mr. Bassett."

Toby ambled lazily over and dropped down on the grass beside Emily. He was wearing a striped rowing blazer with white flannels. He looked like an illustration of something called *My Oxford Days.*

Tilly introduced Emily to him. Toby stared at Emily vaguely and Emily stared wonderingly back. Then the puppy romped in between them, jumping up to lick Toby's face, and then rolled on its back and waved its fat little paws in ecstacy.

"He's called Towzer," said Emily shyly. "It's not a very original name, but he seems to like it." She chattered happily on and Toby seemed content to lie in the sun and listen, his straw boater tilted over his eyes.

Tilly watched her husband's animated face as he talked to the vicar and his wife and wished the moment could be frozen in time— the marquess's fair head gleaming in the sunlight against the cool green background of the trees. The garden smelled of flowers, sugar, cake, and tea. Up above, great white castles of clouds sailed majestically across a cornflower-blue sky. Beyond the wrought-iron gate set into the garden wall, a field of corn stretched lazily into the summer distance, turning green and gold as the breeze rippled across it.

Then the marquess rose to his feet and the golden spell was broken. Toby dusted grass and leaves from his clothes and looked about him in a bewildered way, as if he were emerging from a particularly beautiful dream and wished to stay asleep.

The marquess and Toby, it transpired, had walked the five miles to the vicarage, while Tilly and Francine had traveled in the dog-cart. With a slight hesitation in his voice, the marquess asked Tilly if she felt energetic enough to walk back with him and let Toby and Francine travel in the dogcart. She nodded her assent and unfurled her white lace parasol to protect her face from the sun.

They all left, promising to come again. To Tilly's surprise, the marquess pressed an invitation to dinner at Chennington on the vicar and his family. Toby had that rare sober look on his face as he picked up the reins of the dogcart and bowled off down the dusty lane with Francine sitting beside him, her print cotton dress fluttering in the wind.

The married couple walked along in silence. To take her mind off her disturbing companion, Tilly was turning over in her mind the possibilities of matchmaking. What if Toby should marry the vicar's daughter? Perhaps all he needed was to fall in love with someone and, although Emily was only a country vicar's daughter, Toby's family must know of his excesses and would surely be delighted to see him settled with a respectable girl. If he ever got free of Aileen's clutches!

"Penny for them," said the marquess.

"I was thinking of Toby," began Tilly and then saw a dark scowl on her husband's face. Of all the unfortunate remarks! She hastened to explain. "I was only thinking that perhaps Toby would settle down and not drink so much if he were married to a nice girl like Emily."

"Wouldn't that break your heart?" he demanded acidly, beginning to walk more quickly, so that Tilly had to pick up her skirts and lengthen her step to keep up with him. "He's free now, you know. The engagement's off."

"Oh, do slow down!" she cried. "Please, Philip. I want to talk to you."

The marquess slowed his step, and Tilly caught her breath and gathered her courage. "I only said that about Toby that night to hurt you," she said in a small voice. "I wanted to hurt you the way you had hurt me . . . only making love to me because of the terms of your father's will."

"I should have told you about the will," said the marquess after a long silence, during which poor Tilly thought he would never speak again. "But it seemed so cold, so crude. Especially after my abominable behavior on our wedding night." There, he had said it, and he felt infinitely better. "I wanted to make you fall in love with me, Tilly. That was suddenly the most important thing."

Tilly's heart seemed to stand still. "Why?" she asked. "Why was it so important?"

He stopped, turned, and looked at her. She was wearing a cool white blouse with a lace bertha that had a little ribbon of black velvet threaded through the lace at the neck. A wide biscuit-colored straw hat covered in a whole garden of fruit was perched on her small head, casting her face into shadow. Her long sage-green poplin skirt was tailored tightly over her hips to accentuate her trim figure. The white lacy parasol sent golden flecks of sunshine flickering over her face and dress, and in her wide blue eyes two large, perfect tears formed and welled slowly over onto her cheeks.

He took out his handkerchief and gently dried her tears. "I have fallen in love with you, Tilly," he said slowly. "Perhaps I have always been in love with my noisy schoolgirl and then my beautiful wife. I didn't know it until this minute. I wanted you to be in love with me to satisfy my vanity. But I am in love with you, dear heart."

Poor Tilly broke down and cried, standing in the middle of the dusty country lane with the great tears raining down her face and falling to sparkle on the lace of her blouse. He looked around and saw a few yards in front of them a little stone bridge curving up to cross a glittering stream that ran underneath.

He took her gloved hands in his and led her gently to the parapet of the bridge and made her sit down. Then he dried her tears again, bending his head forward to catch her broken words. "I—I l-love you so awfully, Philip."

He put an arm around her shaking shoulders and hugged her close, murmuring, "Don't cry, sweetheart. Please don't cry. You will ruin your pretty eyes," and other such nonsense that was like a balm to Tilly's soul.

When she had recovered, he turned her face up and kissed her softly on the lips. "I am a beast," he said penitently. "And I scared you and rushed you, didn't I? Listen,

Tilly, I shall make it up to you. You shall have your courtship and your kisses and love letters and flowers, just like any other girl. And then when we—you know—when we feel *comfortable* together, we can get down to some more serious lovemaking. We have all the time in the world now that we know we love each other."

Tilly gave a sigh of pure happiness and leaned her head against his chest, crushing her smart straw hat in the process. They sat like that for a long time, as if turned to stone.

The silver water chuckled over the stones of the river underneath the bridge. The breeze had dropped and tiny blue butterflies danced erratically through the heavy summer air.

Somewhere in the warm distance, Cyril Nettleford espied the two figures and dismounted from his horse, tethered it to a tree, and made his way quickly and cautiously across the fields on foot until he was able to creep down under the shadow of the bridge.

He mopped his streaming face and listened hard.

"You have not answered me, Tilly," the marquess was saying in such a caressing voice that Cyril felt his heart sink to his elastic-sided boots. "Shall we have our courtship and leave the more dramatic side of lovemaking until later?"

"Oh, yes, Philip," sighed Tilly shyly, failing to hear an echoing sigh of relief from under the bridge.

I still have time, thought Cyril. *Sentimental fools.* The well-turned calf of a footman or the trim, muscular waist of a valet could set Cyril's unlovely pulses racing. Women disgusted him.

He crept to the side of the bridge and watched the happy couple make their way off down the road. The marquess stopped, gathered Tilly in his arms, and kissed her hard. The two bodies seemed to fuse together in the dizzying, dancing sunlight.

Blast! thought Cyril cynically. *They won't wait long.* He chewed his lip and thought how convenient it would be if Tilly could meet with an accident. From there his mind moved on to the idea that an accident might be arranged.

Francine was waiting for Tilly when that young lady bounced into her room, looking flushed and exhilarated. She breathlessly told Francine of the marquess's proposed wooing.

"Very much the gentleman," was Francine's delighted comment. "I was wrong about that one. I think now that all men are perhaps not like my wicked compt."

"And, oh, Francine," cried Tilly, throwing her mangled hat on the bed, "I have a marvelous plan for Toby. Wouldn't it be splendid if he were to marry Emily Waring? I am sure she is just what he needs."

"Emily is too young," said Francine repressively.

"Fiddle," sang Tilly, pirouetting around the room. *"I* am much younger than Philip and only see how it has worked out. I want everyone to be happy. What about you, Francine? I feel in the matchmaking mood. What about James, the footman? He is so handsome and I have seen the way he looks at you!"

"James is not for me," said Francine primly. "Just be satisfied with your own happiness, my lady. It is always wrong to meddle in other people's lives. See what a mess I was making with you and your good husband!

"Now come, my lady, I will draw your bath. It is nearly evening and you want to look your best for dinner, *non? Alors,* there is just one little favor I wish to ask, my lady."

"Anything," said Tilly, who felt that if she

could wrap up the world and give it to Francine, she would do it there and then.

Francine cast down her eyes and pleated the material of her print dress in her long fingers. "It is an unusual request, Lady Tilly," she said at last. "You know that I have been in the habit of escorting you to the drawing room before dinner?"

Tilly nodded.

"And always I am very correct. I wear the print dress in the daytime and the black silk at night. *Eh bien,* tonight, to celebrate your happiness, I would like to wear a color. Something very plain. I would not wish to appear not to know my place."

"Of course, Francine," said Tilly, amazed. "I have masses of gowns. Take anything you want. We are now about the same size."

"That is very generous of you, Lady Tilly, but I do have a suitable dress of my own. Your gowns would be too elaborate for a lady's maid."

"As you wish," said Tilly. "Isn't life marvelous, Francine? Nothing can happen to hurt me now."

Tilly had been rejoicing at the thought of only Cyril Nettleford being present that evening, but as she walked into the drawing room it was to find herself faced by two high-nosed, formidable ladies attired in the latest fashions in mauve silk and the latest in hard, frosty stares.

The marquess introduced his aunts, Lady Mary Swingleton and Lady Bertha Anderson. Both were wearing feathered headdresses and, as they nodded their heads to Tilly, they looked remarkably like a pair of well-bred, high-stepping bridling horses. Both had remarkably fine complexions, each appearing to boast a natural, doll-like circle of color on each cheek. Tilly only learned later that the aunts had had the color of their faces tattooed on by no less a practitioner than George Burchett. A faint smell of sweat was still considered attractive to the opposite sex, being called "*Bouquet de Corsage,*" and to Tilly's fastidious nostrils, the aunts appeared to have it in abundance.

"So you're the bride," said Lady Mary, staring down her nose at Tilly's slim figure in its white, demure lace dress. "Saw you at your wedding. You've changed a lot. Hasn't she, Bertha?"

Lady Bertha produced a lorgnette and studied Tilly with a pair of hideously magnified eyes.

"Quite," she said.

"At least she's correctly dressed," barked Lady Mary. "Not like some I could mention."

Both aunts turned as one person and glared at Cyril Nettleford, who was lounging in a chair by the fireplace in a blue velvet smoking jacket. He scratched his spots angrily and stared back.

"My dear," said the marquess, drawing Tilly to him, "my aunts assured me they sent us a wire announcing their arrival and find it hard to believe that we never received it. But you are always unfortunate with your communications, aren't you, Aunt Bertha? My father always swore that you never sent them, but it was probably his idea of a joke. And we have another guest, Tilly. You remember Mrs. Plumb, of course."

Tilly looked carefully around the room. It was like one of those competitions in the illustrated papers—"What Is Up with This Picture?" After some minutes she was able to make out Mrs. Plumb lying on a dark-green sofa, wearing a dark-green dress. Mrs. Plumb smiled faintly and closed her eyes.

Lady Bertha turned her attention to Francine. "You haven't introduced me to the lady," she pointed out.

"My lady's maid, Mademoiselle Francine," said Tilly.

"Indeed!" said both aunts in outraged tones and, as one, they turned their backs on Francine and began talking to Toby Bassett, who was communing with a glass of lemonade over by the windows.

Francine certainly looked every inch a lady —and a very attractive one at that. She wore a deep burgundy silk dress cut low on the bosom and swept up into a bustle at the back. Her black hair was dressed in a looser, less severe style.

"I'm sorry about this, Tilly," said the marquess quietly. "They are very bad-mannered and make a habit of dropping in on people without warning. I shall let them stay for two days and then I'll get rid of them."

"How?" asked Tilly.

"In the usual way," said her husband, smiling. "I shall simply tell the servants to pack their baggage and bring their chariot round, and I'll insist that they told me they were leaving. Mrs. Plumb won't inconvenience us. She sleeps the whole time."

"Where are their husbands?"

"Both dead. But they both have marriageable daughters. It's a miracle they didn't bring them along as well to show me what I'm missing."

"Are they so very pretty?"

"Not as pretty as you, anyway," he said, smiling into her eyes in such a way that Tilly wondered whether a slow, delicate courtship was a good idea after all.

Dinner was served earlier that evening, the host wishing to pack his unwelcome guests off to bed. Lady Bertha, feathers nodding, regaled Tilly with various stories that all seemed to deal with the marquess's soft heart —". . . always helping lame ducks," and ". . . quite a terrible reputation with the ladies, my dear, but I am sure you will keep a *firm eye* on him."

Toby Bassett seemed even more stormy and brooding than ever and was drinking iced lemonade in great gulps. Tilly hoped it was the influence of the pretty vicar's daughter, and when Toby at last joined the conversation with a vague remark that he had once wanted to take holy orders, Tilly was sure of it and quite glared at her husband, who had collapsed in an unmanly fit of the giggles.

Cyril excused himself before the dessert was served. He said he had just remembered that Sir Charles Ponte had asked him to drop over that evening. Sir Charles was a military martinet whose estates bordered the marquess's to the south. Lady Bertha acidly expressed her amazement that a *gentleman* like Sir Charles should wish the company of a young man like Cyril, but Cyril had already left.

Mrs. Plumb was the next to go, protesting faintly that late nights gave her the headache. She seemed unable to stay awake for longer than an hour at a time.

Then the marquess was called to the telephone, which was, as in most country houses, situated in the draftiest and darkest corner of the hall.

He came back looking worried, and bent over Tilly's chair.

"That was some relative of old Crump's," he said. "He's one of my tenant farmers. He has had a heart attack and I really must go and see him. They've called the doctor, of course, but you know how it is, Tilly, in these family emergencies. . . . ?"

"It's all right," said Tilly, her heart sinking. "I will entertain your aunts until you get back."

Then Toby Bassett muttered that he was feeling unwell and begged to be excused, and Tilly was indeed alone with her two formidable tormentors, who proceeded to make the most of it.

In sugary-sweet tones, they recounted all

the marquess's amourous adventures, until Tilly felt ready to sink under the dinner table. In despair, she led them through to the drawing room, hoping for the support of Francine, but the lady's maid was unaccountably absent and Masters, who answered her summons, sent a footman in search of Francine, but that young lady was not to be found anywhere in the great mansion.

I am a married woman, thought Tilly fiercely, *and this is my home. I don't want to endure another minute of these horrible women.* Aloud, she said, "You must excuse me, ladies, but I have a headache and I am going to bed," and before they could open their painted mouths (coral pink—the *latest* shade) to reply, she had left the room.

Tilly bounced into the sanctuary of her sitting room and leaned her back against the door, all that the aunts had told her of her husband's love affairs pounding in her ears. *But that's all over,* she thought. *It must be over.* And then she saw the flowers and the card on the low table in front of the fireplace.

The card was typewritten and carried a brief message: MEET ME OVER BY THE BATCHETT'S SPINNEY AND WE CAN HAVE A FEW MOMENTS TOGETHER. PHILIP.

Even his name was typewritten. Tilly, who

had never seen her husband's handwriting, assumed he was one of those unfortunate people with handwriting that looked as if a drunken spider had staggered over the paper, and he had therefore sensibly resorted to the typewriter, even for the writing of personal notes. The flowers were beautiful deep red roses nestling in a bed of maidenhair fern.

Then she frowned. He hadn't mentioned any particular time but, the evening was beautiful, so it would be pleasant to wait for him, faraway from the house and its contingent of unwanted guests.

She threw a warm cashmere shawl over her shoulders and, still wondering about the whereabouts of the absent Francine, slipped quietly down the stairs and across the hall. The sound of muted conversation filtered from the drawing room. The aunts were hard at it—*No doubt taking my character apart piece by piece,* thought Tilly as she quietly let herself out of the main door. She suddenly realized she did not know the whereabouts of Batchett's Spinney.

An elderly gardner was weeding a rose bed at the side of the drive. He stood up and touched his forelock as Tilly approached. Aye, he kenned fine where Batchett's Spinney was. It was the other side of the Home Wood. Ye couldn't miss it. There was a big swing hanging over a bit pool, where the village bairns had a bit of a swim.

Tilly thanked him and the elderly Scotsman bent once more to his work. It was a beautiful evening with the leafy branches of the Home Wood stretching up to a tender green sky that faded to pale pink near the horizon. Birds chirped sleepily from the trees and vague rustlings from the undergrowth showed that the nocturnal animals were already on the prowl. Tilly picked her way carefully through the darkness of the wood. A pheasant suddenly rocketed up in front of her, sending her heart flying into her mouth.

She came out of the wood and found she was standing almost on the edge of the pool, which was fed by a bubbling stream. The pool looked cool and calm, its black surface mirroring the dying light of the sky above. On the far side was a stunted fir tree with one long branch sticking out at right angles high above the pool. On this, someone had suspended a swing by long ropes, the seat of the swing being a worn plank held by large knots. It was tied back against the trunk of the tree at the top of a tall, rough ladder. When released, the swing would dangle out over the pool a good twelve feet above the water. Tilly guessed that the village boys must use it as a diving perch.

There was no sign of the marquess.

Great boulders were piled higgledy-piggledy around the pool, as if thrown down at random by a giant hand. White bramble flowers shone in the gloom of tangled shrubbery beside the water and a stand of wild roses trailed thorny tendrils on the calm surface.

Tilly eyed the swing. Francine would not approve and it would be a tomboyish thing to do, but the lure was irresistible. She climbed gingerly up the ladder, hampered by her long skirts, and untied the knot that held the swing and, seating herself on it, swung out sideways from the tree until she was suspended high above the pool. Tilly was happy just to sit there, high above the ground, drinking in the peace of the evening, waiting for her beloved husband to arrive.

Perhaps he would take her to the seaside, thought Tilly happily. Tilly had never seen the sea, her father preferring to remain immured at Jeebles, letting the world come to him. Tilly remembered how amazed her husband had looked at dinner when she had confessed she did not know how to swim. He probably thought such a tomboy—or *ex-tom-*

boy, Tilly corrected herself severely—would know how to swim. She had been about to ask him if they could not possibly visit somewhere like Brighton, but the aunts had closed in with their malicious remarks and the question had never been put.

The sky deepened to a strange dark green and the first stars began to appear.

Tilly swung dreamily to and fro, the fine lace of her dress fluttering out behind her.

Suddenly she received an enormous shove from behind and seemed to go sailing up, up toward the stars.

She came hurtling back, trees and sky and pool tumbling dizzily before her eyes.

"Philip!" shouted Tilly, half laughing, half screaming. "You are an utter beast! Stop it or I shall land in the water!"

Another massive shove in the middle of her back nearly sent her flying from her perch and she clutched hard at the ropes as the night sky seemed to swing down to meet her.

Her cashmere shawl went fluttering down and lay like a dying swan on the surface of the pool.

As the swing started its dizzying rush back Tilly wildly twisted her head around—and screamed in earnest this time. A creature out of her worst nightmares was crouched halfway up a tree behind the fir that held the swing, so that he could catch it on the backswing. He, or it, was dressed in black, except that where there should have been a human head was a grotesque pink carnival mask fixed in an evil grin.

Another vicious push sent her flying off the seat of the swing and she clung with both hands to one of the ropes, while again the night sky rushed to meet her and the now brightly shining stars flared and danced before her terror-stricken eyes.

In a flash she realized that whoever it was—and dear God, it could not be Philip—planned to throw her forward toward the pool, so that if she did not drown in the pool, she would surely crack her head against the rocks. Poor Lady Tilly, they would say. What a terrible accident!

All this rushed through her mind in a second and as the swing rushed down and back and up toward her assailant she twisted around so that the seat was pointed toward that nightmarish figure.

But it deftly caught the other rope and held on, the nightmarish mask staring into her terrified eyes. Then, in a strange, sibilant, sexless whisper that was to haunt her dreams for many nights to come, the figure said, "You'll soon get tired. Your arms will get so very tired and then you'll drop . . . drop to your *death.*"

Another almighty shove and off and up she went again. The swing was so high above the ground that each massive push seemed to send her flying nearer to the sky.

Tilly found her voice and began to scream. With an acrobatic skill borne of sheer desperation, she caught hold of the other rope at the last minute and swung herself over, drew back her legs, and kicked out with all her might. The grotesque carnival figure crashed back down through the branches and Tilly swung back out, with less momentum this time, hanging on for dear life, screaming and screaming and then hearing an answering shout from the woods.

Slower and slower went the swing until it hung gently over the pool. Now all Tilly had to do was swing gently over to the ladder, climb off, and climb down.

"Tilly!"

The marquess stood on the far side of the pool.

Weak with relief, her trembling arms lost their strength and she let go of the rope and plunged down into the dark waters of the pool.

The weight of her clothes dragged her down, down, down until her feet touched the mud at the bottom and, with what seemed like the last of her senses, she marshaled her forces, bent her knees, and thrust herself up through the black water roaring in her ears, until her head broke the surface. A pair of strong arms grabbed hold of her and she gasped and struggled and fought until she heard her husband's voice saying, "It's me, Tilly. Philip. Relax and don't fight me and I'll have you out of this in a trice." Two swift strokes brought her to the bank, and the marquess pulled his shivering, trembling wife to safety.

At first he could not grasp what she was saying as the frightened words tumbled out of her in an incoherent jumble. At last the story emerged and he wrapped her tenderly in his dry jacket, which he had left on a bush when he had plunged in to rescue her.

"Cyril!" he exclaimed between his teeth. "It *must* have been Cyril. Come on! Back to the house. Let's catch him."

Tilly tried to pull him back. It couldn't possibly be Cyril, that frightening figure in the tree. She wanted to stay secure in the circle of her husband's arms and never leave them.

But he gently urged her back through the wood, forcing her to quicken her steps.

When they reached Chennington, Tilly was bundled upstairs to be bathed and dried with the assistance of a housemaid, since Francine had not reappeared.

The marquess changed rapidly out of his sopping evening clothes into an old jumper and flannels and, striding through the long rooms of his mansion and crying for blood, he demanded the presence of Cyril Nettleford. The aunts were roused from their gossip in the drawing room to startled dismay and exclamations. Even Mrs. Plumb flitted down the stairs like a pale ghost of one of the Heppleford ancestors, and a sober and strangely elated Toby Bassett joined in the hunt.

Cyril was nowhere to be found.

The clanging of the bell at the main door drew all the servants and searchers there. Cyril Nettleford was carried in on a makeshift stretcher. His unlovely face was bruised, cut, and scratched, and his eyes were closed.

"What the hell happened to him?" demanded the marquess of the two farm laborers who were carrying him in. "Fell out of a tree?"

"No, my lord," vouchsafed one of the men,

shuffling his feet and tugging his forelock. "Mr. Nettleford was lying in the ditch. That there dogcart was overturned with 'er side all stove in. Reckon he hit his head on a rock."

Cyril opened his eyes and grinned faintly. "Sorry to be a bore," he whispered. "Something startled the horse and it reared up and overturned the dogcart. I'm just shaken. No bones broken."

"Where were you?" demanded the marquess.

"I was at the corner of the road, just outside the main gates," said Cyril in hurt surprise. "I don't see why you must go on at a fellow like this. I'm sorry about your carriage, but it wasn't my fault. I was on my road back from Sir Charles Ponte's place. Don't look at me like that. If you don't believe me, telephone the old boy."

"I shall do just that," said the marquess. He gave a sovereign to the gratified farm laborers, who assisted Cyril to a chair beside the hall fireplace and took their leave.

The marquess strode toward the telephone and picked up the heavy earpiece and told the exchange to connect him with Sir Charles.

To his surprise, Sir Charles immediately confirmed that Cyril had only left the place a

219

bare half hour ago. "Yes, yes, yes," bawled Sir Charles jovially, "was with me all the time, what. That what you want to know?"

The marquess thanked him and slowly put the earpiece back on the stand. It *must* have been Cyril. And yet, now it seemed as if there was no possible way Cyril could have been attempting to kill Tilly, for, at the crucial time, he was evidently at Sir Charles Ponte's.

Complaining sulkily over his harsh treatment and saying that Philip should at least have the grace to apologize, Cyril was assisted off to bed, casting many a languished glance at James, the footman, as that young man helped him up the stairs.

Tilly shrank back against the banister as he was helped past. She then listened in growing fright to the marquess's tale of Cyril's innocence. "Don't worry, my dear," he added anxiously, seeing the large tears running down Tilly's face, "we shall telephone the police in the morning and they will get to the bottom of this. Never fear."

"It's not that," wailed Tilly, handing him a note. "This was on my dressing table. Francine has left me and she doesn't even say why."

The marquess silently read the note. It was very brief. Francine presented her regrets to

Lady Tilly, but wished to terminate her employment on the spot. Milady was not to worry about her. She was well and happy.

"And that's not all," cried Tilly. "That note I told you about. The typewritten one. It's gone! Even the flowers have gone. Oh, my poor head. Do you think I imagined the whole thing?"

He shook his fair head slowly, still staring down at the note. "There was nothing up with old Crump either," he remarked bitterly. "So my telephone call was a hoax as well. Someone wanted me out of the way while he tried to murder you."

There was a long silence. One of the servants had lit the fire in the hall and it crackled merrily. All the clocks in the great house began to chime the midnight hour, from the deep bong-bong-bong of the grandfather clocks downstairs to the silvery tinkle of the French clocks in the salons on the first floor.

"Well, I must say," twittered Lady Bertha, "nothing like this would have ever happened at dear Chennington before."

"So *sad,*" sighed Lady Mary. "I feel as if the peace of one of England's greatest homes has been broken forever. . . ."

The elegant Lady Tilly disappeared in a

flash and the old tomboy emerged as Lady Tilly rounded on the aunts in a fury.

"Oh, go to bed, you troublemaking old frumps!" she yelled.

"That's the stuff, Tilly!" said Toby Bassett, grinning.

"And don't say you've never been so insulted," pursued Tilly, her face flushed and her bosom heaving, "cos with your rotten, spiteful manners I'm sure you have, *many times!*"

"Well!" was all the bridling and snorting aunts could muster, their feather headdresses shaking with rage.

"Quite right, my dear," came the faint voice of Mrs. Plumb from a dark corner, startling them all. "Mary and Bertha were always a nuisance, even as gels. I remember when you, Bertha, wanted to run off with that waiter from Brown's Hotel and you, Mary—"

But that was as far as she got. With a frantic rustling of silk skirts, the aunts fled to the safety of their rooms.

The marquess put an arm around his wife's shoulders and led her into the drawing room. Toby followed silently behind.

They sat in silence for a few moments and then the marquess spread out Francine's letter, which he had crushed in his hand. "You don't think," he said slowly, "that it could have been a woman up that tree? I mean, someone could have been paying Francine . . ."

Tilly angrily shook her head. "Francine's the best friend I ever had. She would never do anything to hurt me. That note may be a forgery."

Masters was sent to bring down Francine's book, which itemized the contents of Tilly's jewel box and lace safe, and the handwriting in the book exactly matched that of the note.

Masters coughed discreetly. "The dogcart has been taken round to the stables, my lord. The horse has sustained no hurt. I cannot understand it, my lord. The horse was Dapple, a very mild-mannered gelding."

"Thank you, Masters," said the marquess. "That will be all. No, wait a bit. Bring us something to drink."

"May I suggest champagne, my lord?" said Masters. "A couple of bottles of Dom Pérignon would have a soothing, yet enlivening effect."

"Just so," replied the marquess with a ghost of a smile. "By all means let us be soothed and enlivened."

Tilly stared miserably at her husband. Everything had been so perfect and now it was all spoiled by this brooding fear. Her husband looked heartbreakingly handsome as he lay back in his chair, with the soft glow from the lamp beside him gilding his hair, the faded blue of his jumper bringing out the startling blue of his eyes.

The arrival of the champagne caused a little bustle. Toby looked at it thoughtfully, but to everyone's surprise, declined.

"Something happened to me at the vicarage," he said. "I suddenly thought I might settle down and get married myself, and no nice girl would want a fellow around who was always drunk."

Despite her misery, Tilly could not refrain from flashing a triumphant look at the marquess. So Toby had fallen for the pretty Emily after all!

"I may leave for London tomorrow," went on Toby. "I'll pop into the vicarage before I go. There's something I want to see the old man about. You know, I don't suppose any of us feel sleepy with all this mystery. I, for one, would love to take a stroll down the drive to take a look at that place where Cyril was supposed to have overturned."

"Waste of time," said the marquess gloomily. "Sir Charles isn't the sort to lie. As a matter of fact, it's a miracle the old martinet could even bear Cyril's company for two seconds, let alone a whole evening!"

"Oh, let's go!" said Tilly suddenly, finding the effects of the champagne were all that Masters had promised. "I can't sleep. I feel I want to do *something.*"

"Very well," said her husband, getting to his feet. "It's a fine night and a walk will probably do us all good. I'm amazed at your stamina, Tilly."

Tilly suddenly wondered if he would have preferred her to be more feminine, more weak and ailing. *But, goodness knows,* thought poor Tilly, *I couldn't be more frightened!*

CHAPTER TEN

Stars burned and blazed above in a deep, dark sky as the threesome made their way down the long drive. The air was cool and sweet and heavy with the scent of grass and flowers. But somewhere in this garden of English Eden lurked a serpent, and that thought seemed to make the very peace of the night sinister.

They walked out into the road, chalky white in the moonlight; moonlight so bright that every small pebble cast a small, sharp-edged black shadow.

Toby held up the lantern as they moved slowly along. "This'll be it," he said at last. "Look at those bits of broken wood in the ditch. Funny the dogcart should have been so smashed up. There are only those two rocks and they're pretty smooth."

The three stood and studied the scene of the accident in silence.

There was nothing to see except a few pieces of polished wood, lying in thin splinters on the shaggy, dew-laden grass at the edge of the road.

"Let's go back . . ." the marquess was beginning, when Tilly screamed in pure terror. "There's something watching us from behind that tree," she cried. "I saw its eyes in the moonlight. It's *horrible.*"

The marquess shoved her into Toby's arms and plunged into the woods in the direction she had pointed. There was the sound of a scuffle, then a sharp protest, and then the marquess appeared, dragging behind him what appeared to be a furious bundle of rags.

Revealed by the moonlight, an old tramp stood wriggling in the marquess's grasp.

"Leggo, guv," he protested. "You're a-breaking of me arm."

"I'll break a lot more than your arm, fellow," said the marquess, giving him a shake. "What the bloody hell do you mean by spying on us?"

"I didn't mean nothin', guv," whined the tramp. "I was asleep and I 'eard your gentry voices, like, so I says to meself, I says, they're still maybe playin' games, like, and maybe if I'm smartish, they'll give me sumpin' as well."

"We are not playing games. We are—What do you mean, give you something as well?"

"Like the other cove did. Leggo, you're a-hurtin' me."

The marquess relaxed his grip. "Look, my man, a gentleman claims he had an accident at this corner. Did you see it?"

"'Appen I did," said the tramp with a slow grin.

"Well, tell us! Out with it!"

"'Ow much?"

"Oh, you conniving rascal. Here!" The marquess dug in the pocket of his venerable flannels and pulled out two sovereigns. "No, you don't," he said as the tramp made a grab at the gold. "Story first."

"Well, it be like this," said the tramp. Tilly, shivering in Toby's arms, wondered vaguely why he smelled of her own perfume and then forgot it as the tramp began to speak.

"This 'ere gentry cove," went on the tramp, "I seen 'im right 'ere and 'e 'ad this carriage on its side, like, and 'e was a-stovin' the side in with a rock. 'E sees me and 'e says like 'ow it's a bit of a joke and 'ow 'e'll give me a guinea for to keep me peepers closed,

229

so to speak. Right, guv, says I, thinking as 'ow there's no 'arm in a fellow breaking up 'is own carriage cos, savin' your presence, guv, the swells do get up to some nifty goings-on. I 'member the time young Lord—"

"Enough!" The marquess handed him the money. "Now, take yourself off. You're quite right. It was only a joke after all."

"I say, Philip," protested Toby, "hadn't you better keep tabs on him? He'll be needed as a witness."

"'Ere, not me!" cried the tramp, alarmed. "I ain't 'aving the rozzers after me." And with that, he plunged back into the trees with amazing agility.

"Let him go," said the marquess as Toby tried to follow. "We shall telephone Sir Charles . . . no, no . . . we'll *call* on him and get to the bottom of this. I shall deal with Cyril myself. My name has been bandied about the press enough as it is. Cyril must have faked the accident to account for the cuts and bruises he received when Tilly kicked him out the tree."

It took another three quarters of an hour before the marquess's brougham, driven by a sleepy coachman, deposited them in front of Sir Charles's mansion. It was a big, brooding, ugly barracks of a place, the windows shuttered and eyeless against the still night.

After what seemed like ages of pounding on the door and ringing the bell, a footman, half in and half out of his livery, answered the door. He was just protesting that he would not dare disturb his master at such a late hour of the night when a candle flickered on the staircase behind him and the majestic figure of Sir Charles Ponte could be seen descending, despite his attire of long flannel nightshirt, red wooly nightcap, and morocco slippers.

"I'm sorry to disturb you, Sir Charles . . ." began the marquess.

"So I should damn well think," roared Sir Charles. "That you, Heppleford? Well, I must say this is too much by half. I'm a good sort. I like party games and all that twaddle myself and I'm willing to play along, but not if it means I'm to be rousted from my bed in the middle of the deuced night. Is that right, or isn't it right?" demanded Sir Charles, betraying a surprising knowledge of the current small talk, where repeating questions was all the rage.

"It isn't a party game," said the marquess patiently. "And I certainly wouldn't get you out of bed on such a trivial matter. I simply want to know if Cyril Nettleford was here this evening."

"Well, isn't that just what I've been saying?" roared Sir Charles. "Course he was here."

Three hearts sank.

"And I must say," went on the enraged Sir Charles, "I would have thought at your age, Heppleford, you would have got over these schoolboyish pranks. Murder, indeed! Pah!" he added, with true Palmerstonian vehemence.

The marquess stiffened. "Look, Sir Charles," he said in a quiet, tense voice. "I am not playing silly buggers. I am in deadly earnest. Someone attacked Lady Tilly tonight and I believe that person to have been Cyril Nettleford. But he claims he spent the evening with you and now you confirm it. And what's this about murder?"

"Well, I'll be damned!" exclaimed Sir Charles, scratching his gray hair and knocking his nightcap to the side of his head in the process. "You'd better come in. Bassett's with you, I see. Dear, dear, dear. Lady Tilly? Oh, my stars and garters! Here, Henry, fetch my dressing gown. Here's a how-de-do," he remarked, unconsciously Gilbertian. "Come in! Come in!"

They followed him into a small salon and waited impatiently, for Sir Charles would not talk until his nightshirt was hidden from the modest gaze of Lady Tilly in the enveloping folds of a huge brown dressing gown.

"Now," he barked. "This is what happened. That creature Nettleford turns up here. Don't like the fellow. Never have. But he's a relative of yours, Heppleford. He says you're all playing a game of Murder and he's the murderer and part of the game is to establish an alibi. He says you will phone me late in the evening and ask me if he's been here and I'm to say yes. That's all. I was so relieved the bounder wasn't staying, I agreed. Anything to get rid of him, don't you know, or don't you? What a business. I'll call the magistrate right away."

"No," said the marquess slowly. "I'll handle this myself. And I would be deeply indebted to you, Sir Charles, if you would forget about the whole thing. We don't want to stand in court and suffer the consequent publicity for a worm like Cyril."

"That's the stuff, my lad!" said Sir Charles enthusiastically. "Horsewhip the cur!"

They rose to take their leave, Tilly shaken, relieved, and disappointed all at once. She was glad the mystery of her attacker was solved, but she would have loved to have seen Cyril in the dock at the Old Bailey.

When the threesome reached home again, Tilly was told firmly to go to bed and stay there and to put the pillow over her ears if necessary. The marquess and Toby Bassett went off to Cyril's rooms.

Tilly lay awake for a long time, wincing as sinister thumps and bangs echoed through the silent house. *I'll never sleep again,* she thought. *Never!* And on that thought she plunged far down into a long and dreamless sleep, while at the other end of the corridor the honor of the Hepplefords was being well and truly avenged.

Tilly descended the stairs on a bright, sunny morning to find the house still and quiet. She felt very cold and slightly sick, a reaction to her experience of the night before.

Mr. Masters, Mrs. Judd, and Mrs. Comfrey were waiting for Tilly in the morning room, bursting with news. His lordship, they said, had gone to pack Mr. Cyril off to Singapore and had even said he was going to buy him a forty-four pound first-class ticket, whereas, in the opinion of the three upper servants, Master Cyril should have been sent steerage. His lordship had also sent his aunts packing and told them not to show their faces at Chennington again until they could show a proper respect for his wife. Mrs. Plumb had also left.

"But is that *all* that's going to happen to Cyril?" asked Tilly, amazed.

"Of course," said Mrs. Comfrey. "You don't want no scandal, my lady. It's always the best thing. Send 'em to the Colonies and let 'em try their evil tricks on the heathens. I don't hold with all them courts and newspapers and things. Best to do things in the good old way."

Mr. Masters coughed delicately. "I may add, my lady," he said, "that Mr. Cyril had two of the most lovely black eyes you ever did see."

"And Mr. Bassett?"

"He's gone to the vicarage and from there he said he was going to London," said Mr. Masters. "His lordship said to tell you to rest, my lady, and that he would be back this evening."

"And Francine?" asked Tilly quietly. "Where is Francine?"

Three heads shook and three faces looked at her with sympathy. "We don't know," said Mrs. Judd. "Leastways she said nothing to nobody here about leaving. You never can tell with them Frenchies, you know. Flighty, that's what."

"I suppose I had better hire a lady's maid," said Tilly.

"If I might make a suggestion, my lady," said Mrs. Judd, "I happen for to know that Lady Archison's lady's maid is not happy in her position, and she's a wonder with hair."

Tilly smiled faintly. "I need someone to do something with my hair. I've been spoiled by Francine. I look like a schoolgirl again."

Mrs. Comfrey shook her head slowly. "No, my lady, that you never will again, if you'll forgive my speaking so plain. You look more natural-like. You don't want to look old before your time, my lady."

But Tilly could not believe her. It was Francine's creation that Philip had fallen in love with and she was frightened of losing him.

During the long afternoon of his absence, she worked and slaved on her appearance with the help of one of the housemaids.

By early evening, when the dressing gong rang, she was already primped and curled and painted and corseted and thoroughly miserable. She dismissed the housemaid and looked at herself in the long glass.

An enameled, fussy stranger stared back at

her. The dress the housemaid had chosen for her was one that Francine had refused to let her wear. It was in Tilly's favorite color, pink, and had a long row of ruffles and velvet bows from throat to hem.

Why on earth did I ever think pink was a good color for me? thought Tilly wonderingly. *This will never do.*

She rang the bell and ordered the surprised housemaid to unfasten the long rows of buttons on the back and to help her out of her dress. Then she demanded cans of hot water and washed and scrubbed the enamel from her face and shampooed the frizz vigorously from her hair. "Oh, my lady," breathed the anguished housemaid, "whatever will Mrs. Judd say to me?"

"Don't care," came Tilly's voice, muffled by her wet hair as it hung in a heavy curtain in front of her face as she knelt before the fire, trying to dry it quickly. Tilly straightened up. "Simply tell Mrs. Judd that you are following my orders."

"Shall we wear the black velvet, my lady?"

"No, we will not," said Tilly. "We will wear that lawn thing Francine gave me."

The housemaid bit her lip in disapproval. Fancy having all these gorgeous silks and satins and settling for lawn. For dinner too!

Tilly finally descended the stairs to wait for her lord, and hearing, with a quickening heartbeat, the sound of carriage wheels on the gravel outside, she rushed quickly into the drawing room and looked anxiously at her reflection in the glass. The lawn dress was of a pale leaf green with a high ruched neckline. It was cut in simple, yet almost severe, lines with long tight sleeves and a straight skirt that just revealed the long, pointed toes of a pair of green openwork high-heeled shoes. Her hair flamed above the high neckline in an unruly mass of shining curls and was secured at the back of her neck by a black velvet ribbon. *Just like a schoolgirl,* thought Tilly, miserably, who knew that a lady, once she had made her coming out, *never* wore her hair down except in the privacy of her bedchamber.

A soft step at the door made her swing around. The marquess stood in the doorway, watching her. His dark-gray suit was impeccably tailored and his waistcoat was a miracle of the embroiderer's art. His tanned, high-nosed face above the hard white of his collar looked unbearably handsome.

"You look . . ." he began. Tilly hung her head. "You look very beautiful," he said with a husky note in his voice that made her heart turn over.

"Come and kiss me, Tilly. It's been too long."

Twenty minutes later Mr. Masters lifted the covers off the dishes on the sideboard in the dining room and then bent to adjust the flame of the spirit lamp under the chafing dish. "Go and ring the gong again, James," he said without turning around. "They can't have heard it."

"Maybe they've got better things to do," said the footman, grinning.

"That's enough from you, young man," said Mr. Masters severely. "Do as you're told!"

Upstairs, my lady's dress whispered from her shoulders to fall at her feet. "God, but you're beautiful," said my lord.

The imperative summons of the gong rang through the house.

"Philip! They're ringing the gong."

"Let them," said the marquess, his voice slightly choked as Tilly's heavy corsets fell to the floor. "I don't think either of us wants a long courtship."

Down in the kitchen, Mrs. Comfrey wrung

her hands as the *soufflé de cailles au riz* began to sink in its pottery dish.

"Ring the gong again, James," said the perturbed Mr. Masters.

"Blimey," said the footman to himself, striding into the hall and picking up the small hammer. "Mr. Masters isn't using his imagination tonight!"

Tilly wound her arms tightly around her husband's neck as he carried her to the bed. "Don't stop kissing me," she whispered. "I'm frightened."

"There's nothing to be frightened of," whispered her husband with his lips against her hair as he lowered her gently onto the bed.

The long row of footmen stood to attention, although the junior members showed an embarrassing tendency to giggle and shuffle. The *boeuf flamande* sizzled impatiently in its chafing dish. Somewhere behind Mr. Master's back, someone sniggered.

"Ring the gong again, James," said Masters.

"But, Mr. Masters, *sir!*"

Mr. Masters swung around. "Do as you're told! If my lord did not wish dinner, then he would have said so!"

The butler and the other footmen waited

in silence as the boom, boom of the gong echoed through the house.

"Philip!"

"What is it, my heart?"

"I can hear the dinner gong. The servants . . ."

"Damn and blast. I forgot. Wait a minute."

James, in the hall, heard the bell ringing from my lady's rooms and leapt to the summons. He got as far as the turn of the corridor and was stopped by the sight of my lord's head sticking around the door at the end. "Oh, James," said the marquess, "we shall not be dining."

"But the food, my lord. Mrs. Comfrey made a special banquet."

"Eat it yourselves and tell Masters you're to wash it down with some bottles of the best."

"Very good, my lord. *Thank you,* my lord."

The marquess slammed and locked the door and returned to more important matters. "Where was I?" he demanded, settling into bed with a sigh of satisfaction. "Ah, yes, I was kissing your left breast. But we must not neglect the right. . . ."

One by one the footmen carried all the splendid dishes back to the kitchen. Mr. Masters unbent enough to order that the table in the servants' hall be laid out with their best china and then went down to the cellars himself to fetch the wine.

Mrs. Judd rushed to put on her best silk dress, and Mrs. Comfrey decided to make another soufflé.

Soon the happy servants were seated around the table. Mr. Masters rose solemnly from his place at the head.

"Ladies and gentlemen," he said, raising his glass. "A toast to my lord and my lady."

And James, carried away by the glory of the occasion, so far forgot himself as to cry out, "Three cheers for Lady Tilly, God bless 'er. Hip! Hip!"

"Hooray!" roared the assembled staff of Chennington.

And so it was that the exultant cries abovestairs, which heralded Lady Tilly's loss of virginity in the great bed, went mercifully unheard.

CHAPTER ELEVEN

A small steamer called *The Alligator* chugged peacefully through the blue waters of the Mediterranean. Cyril Nettleford stretched himself out more comfortably in his long cane deck chair and reflected that things could be worse—much worse. Thank heavens for Heppleford's antique ideas of what was due to his family name. All he could do was hope and pray that Tilly either proved barren or died in childbirth. He, Cyril, could not return to England, of course, since the marquess held his written confession and had promised to use it if he so much as put a foot on English soil again. Cyril blamed himself only for the theatricality of his murder attempt. The mask and the black clothes had given him no end of a sinister thrill. *I should just have pushed her down the stairs,* he thought gloomily. *I always was overly elaborate.*

The sound of shrill female voices approaching made him wince. A certain Miss Cecilia Wendover had been pursuing him from the start of the voyage. Cyril had been unbearably rude to her until the thick-skinned Miss Wendover had casually dropped a remark that Daddy was a rich Singapore merchant, one of the original crusty Scotch settlers who had made a fortune in the opium trade. Cecila was long-nosed and sandy-haired and unbearably arch, but from that moment Cyril began to find her imbued with a mysterious charm.

She prattled on about the "little fishies" and the "sweet natives," and Cyril only heard the music of falling gold coins in her father's counting house. Like Richard III, he had decided to marry her, but not to keep her long.

It would be ideal if he could marry her on board ship and stage an accident before they even reached Singapore. But that way there was no guarantee that he would inherit any money. Father must be met first. Meanwhile, life held promise, his bruises had healed, and the warm sun had reddened his face to match the color of his spots so that they hardly showed. . . .

* * *

Lady Aileen had snared yet another catch of London society in the shape of the Earl of Morningham. It was an Irish peerage, admittedly, but a title for all that, and the earl was undoubtedly handsome and all her friends were envious.

Aileen was entertaining the earl in the Art Nouveau drawing room that had so depressed Tilly. Since she was entertaining her fiancé to tea, she had the luxury of being alone with him. She smiled at him lovingly and he gave her a weak smile back.

"I say, Aileen, old girl," said the earl in a hesitant manner. "It's awfully jolly being alone with you, what . . . I mean not being paraded about in front of your friends like a prize bull."

Aileen stiffened. She poured the Earl Grey into a paper-thin Spode cup with deliberate care. Then she turned a rather steely gaze on her beloved.

"I object to your choice of words, Henry," she said evenly. "I don't parade you about."

"It's not that I blame you," said Henry earnestly. "I mean, after all, what with Bassett disappearing and then there was Heppleford falling for that gorgeous companion of yours . . . well, it stands to reason."

"What stands to reason?" Lady Aileen proceeded to pick little pieces of watercress from her sandwich.

"Well, I mean, after all, jilted twice, what. I mean, got to show the girls you've made it this time."

"Do you think I'm so hard up that I should have to settle for a drip like you?" shrilled Aileen.

"As a matter of fact . . . yes."

"Oh!" Aileen stared at him balefully. The insult was gross. There was only one thing she could do and that was to tell this handsome cad to march. But what would her friends say? Henry looked at her almost hopefully.

"You do not know how cruel and rude you are being," said Aileen at last. "I forgive you."

Henry took a deep breath. "Nothing to forgive," he remarked casually. "Only spoke the truth. May as well make the most of it, old girl, cos you ain't seeing any of those friends of yours after we're married."

"What?"

"Can't stand all this London nonsense," pursued Henry. "Got the place in Ireland, you know. Bit run down and all that, but I like a nice, quiet life."

Aileen made a desperate last stand. She slid along the sofa and wound her arms about his neck. "You can't mean it. You wouldn't take poor little fairy away from London."

"Oh, yes, I would," said Henry calmly. "And another thing. Shouldn't call yourself fairy. Sickening enough when your mother says it."

Aileen gritted her teeth and released him. "Are you trying to force me to break our engagement, Henry?"

"No. But I mean to be master. That's what women are for. You do what I say from now on."

Lady Aileen threw the contents of the teapot at him.

Two days later, London society learned that Lady Aileen was no longer engaged to the Earl of Morningham.

Four days later, Lady Aileen Dunbar appeared at Marlborough Street Magistrates Court, charged with breaking shop windows in Bond Street with her umbrella. Her defense lawyer pointed out that Lady Aileen had just joined the suffragettes movement and was protesting against women not having the vote. She looked very beautiful as she stood in the dock, and did a great deal to further the women's movement. But she was still unwed. . . .

A miserable, chill autumn descended on London, but for some inexplicable reason, Paris was still gilded with sunshine. The Marquess and Marchioness of Heppleford strolled along under the rust-colored leaves of the plane trees on the Champs Élysée.

"Are you sure?" asked the marquess for the umpteenth time.

"Perfectly," said Tilly lazily. "The doctor's sure as well. Oh, won't Cyril be furious. After all his trouble. I hope he doesn't turn up at the christening like a bad fairy."

The marquess stopped at a neighboring news vendor and bought the English papers.

"You are not going to read them in the middle of the street," said Tilly severely. "We shall go to that nice café over there and I can watch the crowds."

The marquess grinned and took her arm and led her toward the nearest café table. Tilly settled back with a sigh of pure contentment.

Then her attention was drawn from the smart boulevardiers and the glossy carriages by an exclamation from her husband.

"Cyril's dead!" he exclaimed, raising his head from a copy of the *Daily Mail*.

"What on earth happened?"

"He fell overboard just before the ship docked at Singapore. There's been a hell of a stink at the inquest. It seems Cyril was entertaining some very handsome purser to drinks in his cabin when they were interrupted by a Miss Cecilia Wendover, who made a hysterical scene. She says she was engaged to Cyril on board ship! She demanded that Cyril come up to the boat deck for a private chat. No one saw the couple after that, but the next thing they knew was that Miss Wendover was running about screaming hysterically and saying that Cyril had fallen overboard. The purser claims she pushed Cyril. But the jury brought a verdict of accidental death. Well!"

"Oh, dear," cried Tilly, her eyes filling with tears. All the horror of that evening on the swing rushed back into her mind.

"Don't worry," said her husband gently. "There will be no more shocks in your life, Tilly. I don't care if Cyril jumped or was pushed. I'm heartily glad he's dead. He's been on my conscience. People who try to kill once may succeed the next time. I had long regretted not having taken him to the police. Don't get so exercised over it, you'll upset the baby," he finished, for Tilly had let out a scream.

"It's not Cyril," said Tilly wildly. "Look who's coming along the road. Only *look!*"

The marquess followed her pointing finger. At first he only saw what appeared to be an English gentleman with a very pretty Frenchwoman on his arm—a not uncommon sight on the boulevards of Paris. Then he too straightened up in amazement as he recognized the couple.

Toby Bassett, with Francine on his arm, came strolling along in a leisurely way in the pale sunlight. Francine was wearing a very modish gown in the latest fashion—a tailored suit by George Poirot in muted green with an otter collar. Over her arm she carried a large otter muff and perched on her glossy curls was a diminutive otter hat. Toby looked the picture of the English gentleman from his well-tailored suit to his glossy top hat.

The couple caught sight of the marquess and Tilly. Toby strode forward, pulling a blushing and embarrassed Francine.

"I say," he cried, waving his cane, "this is splendid. All together again. Meet the wife."

A series of images flashed through Tilly's brain: Francine's print dress fluttering in the breeze as Toby drove her off from the vicarage; Francine asking to be allowed to wear a dress of a different color; Francine transformed and elegant while Toby drank lemonade by the window in the drawing room and the aunts stared; Toby holding her in his arms as she, Tilly, had stood at the side of the road, frightened by the tramp and wondering why Toby smelled of her perfume. Francine used the same fragrance, she suddenly remembered.

"You're married?" asked Tilly faintly as the couple sat down beside them. Tilly had never quite got over her disappointment on finding out that the pretty Emily was unwed and that the mysterious Mr. Bassett had disappeared.

"What's that?" countered Toby vaguely, his eyes losing their focus. He was back in his old state of not quite drunk, not quite sober. Tilly flashed an accusing look at Francine, who got to her feet again.

"We will walk a little way together, Lady Tilly," said Francine, "and leave the gentlemen to their newspapers."

Tilly mutely allowed herself to be led away. Francine stopped at a bench under a plane tree and motioned Tilly to sit down beside her.

"You are shocked, *non?*" demanded Francine.

"I am a bit," said Tilly. "You might have told me."

"You might not have approved, and my lord would certainly have not. And, oh, those aunts! *They* would have had something to say. I had a chance and I took it," said Francine simply. "He was so eager. We were married by special license by your good vicar."

"But Emily—"

"Emily made a very pretty bridesmaid," said Francine.

"Do you love him?" asked Tilly wonderingly.

"No, not in the way you love your lord."

"But he is *drunk* again," protested Tilly hotly. "If he loved someone, he might reform."

"I said I do not love him, but he certainly loves me," said Francine calmly. "And that one will never reform. For my sake, he only gets drunk once a day and that is as much as I can hope for. We will soon go home and he will sleep, and he will be recovered by the evening."

"But why did you marry him? I don't understand," wailed Tilly.

"Why? You ask me, Francine, why? And

after you have worked as a kind of servant yourself," exclaimed Francine. "I am French and infinitely practical. A handsome young man offers me marriage and security. In return, he gets an affectionate keeper. I am a very good wife."

But Tilly only bit her lip. When they returned to join the two men, she still felt upset. Francine was surely no more than a scheming adventuress.

She voiced this disturbing thought when she was safely back in the apartment with her husband. "I think it's answered very well," he said, removing his tie and loosening his collar stud. "Toby's as happy as he can manage to be because Francine does not expect him to change. People don't change, you know. If Toby had married Emily, she would have been a very upset young lady by now. Can you imagine? Her husband falling drunk out of the family pew on Sundays?"

"You say people don't change," said Tilly sadly. "Does that mean you are going to go back to chasing other women?"

He came forward and began to loosen the pins from her hair. "I couldn't go chasing *other* women," he said, "before I met you, that is. I only chased after women. Now I'm perfectly happy to confine my chasing to you." He reached for the buttons at the top of her dress.

"What are you doing?" cried Tilly, trying to button them up again. "It's still daylight!"

"Have you never heard of love in the afternoon?"

"It doesn't seem quite right."

"What if I do this . . . and . . . this . . . and this."

"I can't stop you when you do that to me," moaned Lady Tilly as she was carried into the bedroom. "Oh, rats! You are a beast, Philip!"

Enter the world of regency England
with Marion Chesney, writing

Regency Romances
as Jennie Tremaine.

☐ **DAISY** Daisy Jenkins never expected to be admitted into
the magic world of nobilty until she meets her real father and
discovers she's a lord's daughter! 11683-X $2.95

☐ **GINNY** Ginny Boggs, the daughter of a coal merchant,
must prove that she is a real lady when she inherits a fortune
from an aristocratic benefactor. 12820-X $2.95

☐ **LUCY** By winning a fortune at baccarat, lady's maid Lucy
Balfour connives her way into London's most exclusive society
and tries to win a handsome Viscount's heart! 15609-2 $2.95

☐ **MOLLY** Molly Maguire is a willful American with the brains,
beauty and bravery to conquer London society. But will the
stubborn Lord David Manley eventually conquer her?
15856-7 $2.95

☐ **POLLY** Pretty Polly Marsh always knew she could use her
beauty as a passport into the circles of nobility where she felt
she belonged. But would it get her the affections of the eligible
Lord Peter? 17033-8 $2.95

Special Offer
Buy a Dell Book
For only 50¢.

Now you can have Dell's Readers Service Listing filled with hundreds of titles. Plus, take advantage of our unique and exciting bonus book offer which gives you the opportunity to purchase a Dell book for *only 50¢*. Here's how!

Just order any five books at the regular price. Then choose any other single book listed (up to $5.95 value) for just 50¢. Use the coupon below to send for Dell's Readers Service Listing of titles today!

 DELL READERS SERVICE LISTING
P.O. Box 1045, South Holland, IL. 60473

Ms./Mrs./Mr. _____

Address _____

City/State_____ Zip _____

DFCA - 12/87